AUTHOR BIOGRAPHY

Born in Harrow; living and educated everywhere else.

Since leaving school, Chris has worked in the Opal mines of Australia, completed a nursing course, did a surgical residency at Darwin Hospital; then as a journalist and war correspondent, visited the four corners of the earth. He has achieved an MD, an MA in the English Language, and another complete MA in Woodworking – three of his main vocations.

A horrendous accident in 2009 ended his career in the construction industry, limiting his time to reading and writing.

He now resides in Norfolk where he loves natural history and the countryside.

Christopher E Howard, MA. MD. .a.

This book is dedicated to

The dreamers amongst you
who like to have their favourite tales
in physical form.

I have collated these ebooks together
to present them for you all
to have and to hold.

IV

Lost in R.E.M.

And other stories
By
Christopher E. Howard

Contents

Lost in R.E.M.
and other stories

Author's note; Lost in R.E.M.

What can I say about this novella that hasn't been said before? This one little story has gained me more kudos and notoriety than any other of the time, being reprinted countless times. It's spawned many other stories and films; a pop group; and has been used in medical discussions when oneiromancy ever raises its head. When it appeared over three decades ago, it seemed to break new ground. Fan mail poured in from all over the world, as far away as Japan, Australia and the United States and I'm proud to present it here again now, more or less in its original format.

Sleep tight!

Lost in R.E.M.

First published in *Dream magazine* July 1989 – Trevor Jones

Blinding sunlight sparkled through the windows above, flashing on and off as the framework baulked its radiant beams. Lymhal Morey was enjoying his journey through the empty street. Familiar voices shouted at him from both sides but Lymhal was revelling in the sensation too much to be distracted. He was aware that he had no shape or form; seemed to be just a collection of senses travelling along, carefree, bemused.

He heard a voice he recognised and without intention or impulse found himself making a swinging right turn and swirling down a narrow boulevard. A flash of sunlight and Lymhal was standing in an empty room. He had regained his body.

There was no need to look down at it. Lymhal was aware he was dreaming, even in his dream. He shoved his hands into his pockets and turned to look around.

"Hello, Lymhal…"

Lymhal smiled. Leaning in a doorway was the girl of his dreams.

It was a strange appraisal now that he thought of it. For a start, this one was too crafty, domineering and pert. He would have preferred a girl of his dreams to be more servile and receptive. It showed whenever he tried to conjure a situation in which she would want him desperately, or in which they were destined to couple. She always thwarted his plans. The dreams were always a shambles or hotchpotch of scenes and experiences.

Her hair too was wrong. Lymhal would have liked long wavy hair; instead hers was yellower than he cared for and cut in a shaggy unkempt style, no longer than his own. He smiled at her and continued to stare. (It was, after all, only a dream, and even if she disappeared in a puff of sunlight, it was no great loss.) But Lymhal was perplexed. He realised the dream was more vivid than usual and he was experiencing a slight discomfort inside at not having spoken to her yet. Why, he wondered, had the scene not dissipated or changed into something else when he was only paying it scant attention?

"Aren't you going to say hello today," she asked?

Lymhal laughed. It seemed ludicrous. He had indeed spoken to this very same girl several times in his dreams, in fact, she'd appeared with annoying regularity these last few weeks and Lymhal had wondered if it bore any relation to his real life. She bore no resemblance to anyone he knew and certainly not to any unattainable media personality or film star, she was not the purgative cure to some hankering by autosuggestion.

"It's a nice top," he commented, indicating the chiffon blouse she wore. It should have been see-through, as Lymhal could make out the sides and curvature of her waist; but she had foxed him again by somehow blocking out the parts that clung to her breasts with a soft white light. He contemplated the darker slacks and sandals and smiled.

"This is a pleasant dream," he decided to tell her.

"You should come more often," and she turned to go.

"Wait! Your name?"

"Cherry," she called, turning in the doorway.

"I'll look out for you," he laughed and caught the humorous smirk on her lips too.

The room was vanishing, breaking up into a mess of white and grey. The walls flickered… and Lymhal was awake.

He stretched under the covers and yawned languidly. The time display atop his bedside cabinet read eleven fifteen. Sunlight danced erratically about the curtains as they billowed in an offshore breeze. Lymhal was reluctant to get up. Relaxed and fresh and unperturbed by the time, the warmth of the sheets was something to relish and outweighed any guilt at having missed such a large part of what was obviously a beautiful day.

So content was he that he may well have laid in for some considerable time and even perhaps drifted off back to sleep, but for footsteps on the landing outside and a peremptory knock at the door.

His parents stood in the doorway, his mother buttoned up in a heavy coat, clutching a handbag, despite the warm sunny weather; his father behind her, overdressed also in a three-piece suit and reefer befitting his banking metier.

"Hey, this is a surprise," exclaimed Lymhal, standing aside! "What are you doing over here on a Friday?"

"It's a bank holiday weekend," intoned his father stiffly, following his wife into the room, "or had you forgotten?"

"Really, I guess I must have lost track of the days lately!"

His father grimaced and stood in the centre of the bed-sit looking for a place to sit down. Lymhal cleared the sofa and took their coats, laying them on the bed. "Coffee," he asked?

"We've had some thanks," answered his mother, arranging a decorative neckerchief. She settled into the sofa.

Lymhal forwent the coffee, sitting on the bed opposite.

"So, over to do some shopping, eh?"

"Well, yes, we'll have a look around the shops now we're here, but that's not why we've come." Mother glanced anxiously at father.

"Actually son," started his father, obviously feeling it was his duty to disclose the reason behind the visit, "your mother and I are very concerned about your health."

"My health," laughed Lymhal? "I've never felt better."

"But it's not right," interposed his mother, "living the way you do. Discos and parties every night, sleeping all day; you'll ruin your system."

"It's only a phase; it'll pass."

"You said that last year," his father reminded him.

"Yes, well…" and Lymhal sensed an age-old argument rearing its ugly head.

"Have you sold anything yet" his mother asked glancing around pensively at the canvasses of grey and white abstract designs that he intended to rock the art world with?

"Er no, not exactly; but there's an exhibition coming up soon and I've been given a small area. I've got a couple of people interested."

His parents sighed inwardly. They'd heard it all before.

He shifted uneasily on the bed.

He was sorry now that he hadn't any good news for them, even to say that he was working again would have buoyed them somewhat, but Lymhal hadn't been near the employment agency, had shunned work even when offered it. He was an artist damn it, and artists didn't stack shelves in supermarkets or can baked beans in a factory, not if they wanted to keep their dignity they didn't. The fact that this artist took money from the state was something he'd rather not discuss; they'd get it all back when he made it anyway.

"Lymhal," said his mother, taking on formal tones, "we want you to go away for a while."

"Away! Where..?"

"Well, it's a sort of holiday really, a health farm, get you back on your feet."

Lymhal clamoured for words. "You're joking. How the hell am I going to pay for it?"

"That's already been settled," put in his father. "The manager is an old acquaintance of mine and he's doing this as a favour as you're our son."

"But Mum, Dad, you don't understand. I like to lay in. I dream more vividly and the dreams inspire my work. Some of the greatest artists ever known used the material of their dreams. Coleridge; Edgar Allen Poe; and Dali: The German chemist Kekule envisaged the structure of the benzene ring in a dream – and what about Beethoven – he practically slept on his problems."

"You'll still be able to dream, Lymhal. Mr. Mayhew is just going to get you back on track, back into a proper routine."

"Do you good, boy, get some fresh air into you: Living in a place like this all the time, never venturing outside? It's a wonder you know what time of the day it is."

Lymhal noted the resentment. His father had opted to move to an open plan estate on the advice of their doctor due to troublesome allergy problems, and now they considered the enclosed streets and parks of the mini cities unhealthy and stuffy, even if they were coastal. Lymhal pushed himself off the bed and wandered around the room, stopping by one of his portraits and daubing absently with a charcoal he'd picked up from an ashtray beneath.

"How long is this holiday going to last," he asked?

"It depends on what Mr Mayhew says. A week to two weeks is usually enough, but in your case it may take a little longer."

'Jeeze', thought Lymhal, *'two weeks'*! It was a long time to leave the bed-sit unattended. He sighed and studied the picture. It was one belonging to a friend that he'd started months ago and never got round to finishing, but now that he looked at it, he realised it resembled Cherry, the girl in his dreams.

He squared it up experimentally with his thumbs and found the cheekbones a little too high.

"What am I going to do about my money? I have to sign on next week you know."

"You can get it transferred, but I'd rather you enter a holiday form and have the money there when you want it. There are plenty of outlets. There's no need to let on to Mayhew that you're unemployed. Tell him you are on a grant or something."

Lymhal smiled. Poor Dad; caught so securely on the hook of social standing. He stood back and stared at the now corrected portrait.

It looked remarkably like Cherry, especially now that he had added thick black swirls to emphasise the loose shingle curls of her hair. Lymhal tossed down the charcoal and scrutinised his work.

"Someone we know," his mother asked?

"No; no one really."

"Right," said his father. "Your mother wants to look around the shops so you had better come along. We'll get you some new shirts and things; don't want you turning up at Hedliegh in jeans and God knows what."

"You haven't told me when I'm supposed to be going?"

Once again mother glanced apprehensively at father. Lymhal experienced a sinking feeling.

"Well, actually, we hoped you'd come along this weekend."

"Oh, mum – I'm not packed or anything!"

"We'll get you everything you need at the shops, Lymhal. Don't want you taking any of that old stuff."

Lymhal sighed. It was pointless to argue; might as well get it over with and keep mum happy by going along. *'Who knows'*, he thought *'might even be fun. Could be plenty of girls there!'*

"You go on. I'll have to notify the landlord and see a few people. Meet you back here in an hour or two.

Hedliegh lay along the same coastline, fifty miles to the South, devoting its entire acreage to healthy outdoor activities and employing most of the room in the stately old manor in the pursuit of physical culture and sensible rest and recreation. Annexed to the mansion, a more modern building hugged one side, offering such facilities as a spacious swimming pool, indoor games courts, and so on.

Lymhal shivered as he looked out over the landscape, dotted as it was with the odd shack and farm building, defunct now the estate had fallen into the hands of an entrepreneur. He squirmed in his seat. On his insistence the vehicle's heater was on full and all the vents closed. Around him was wrapped his faithful old sheepskin, an amulet to the vast open spaces.

But if keeping fit and following a strictly controlled diet was part of what Mr Mayhew advocated, then Lymhal wondered if he shouldn't practise what he preached.

The car slowed to a stop outside the manor's main entrance and they all climbed out to stare up at the monstrous building.

"Impressive, eh," commented his father, admiring the pseudo-Georgian architecture? "Don't build 'em like this anymore."

"Thank god," muttered Lymhal, following his parents up the steps.

Inside it all seemed a bit unreal. The massive entrance hall was adorned with huge Arabian vases housing larger and even more riotous pot plants, while taking centre stage was a large gilt-worked fountain with statues of Greek gods and goddesses in the niches. The floor was richly carpeted and big idyllic paintings – garishly framed – and executed,

Lymhal judged, by local artists, filled the ghastly wastes of the walls.

Mayhew, short and fat, decked in a brightly coloured tracksuit bounced into the foyer from an adjoining corridor.

"John! Good to see you. Joan, you're looking well. So this is the young artist, eh? We'll, soon have you back on your feet within a few days. Some careful exercise, plenty of fresh air and good natural food; have you feeling wonderful in no time."

Lymhal wasn't so sure. As he watched Mayhew shake hands vigorously with his mother, he realised he enjoyed life as it was. He slept well, albeit somewhat out of synchronisation with nature, enjoyed a reasonable diet, and he felt remarkably healthy to boot.

As Mayhew babbled on, Lymhal soon recognised him as one of the gin and tonic tubbies of the fashionable sports centres and parks, who could be found in any respectable establishment – usually at the bar! Their total commitment to the improvement of their cardiovascular system consisted of a quick round of golf or game of badminton, which usually left them gasping for breath as they were helped back to the bar by other fine colleagues. Lymhal didn't take any form of regular exercise himself but was proud of his stamina with his many consorts and to that end had nothing bad to say about the permissive society in which he lived. The irony of it all was that Mayhew was getting fat and rich while his clients flogged themselves to death in his emporium.

Lymhal listened for a while to Mayhew's exhortations on the booming health trade, then after kissing his mother, and shaking hands with father, excused himself politely asking to be shown to his room.

It was sparsely furnished and after a cursory glance out of the window, he unpacked and went off to explore.

****

Someone was shaking him. Lymhal woke the next morning and tried to rise but found the theta rhythms of stage three sleep pulling him back.

"Come on, laddie," urged a soft but firm Scottish voice. "Dear me, I can see I'll have to adjust the volume of your alarm a little. It's obviously going to need more than a little buzz to wake you in the morning."

Lymhal sat up wearily and, through uncooperative eyes, watched the matron – a plump middle-aged woman – throwing back the curtains.

He'd read the syllabus with growing horror the day before in one of the many sun lounges. His day was to start at seven o'clock sharp with a twenty-minute exercise period before breakfast, preferably a light bit of jogging – the resident physician, a one Doctor Baines – had advised beforehand during an obligatory medical. At nine he was to report to the gym for some rigorous circuit-training – at which point Lymhal was wishing he'd kept his big mouth shut about just how wonderful he felt. Half-hours' break mid-morning and a joint bout of yoga and aerobics took him through to lunch. He was encouraged to join in on some form of recreation in the afternoon too, but that wasn't necessary for the first week in his case, and he began to wonder if this loop in his programme might allow an afternoon nap, although the afternoons were in practice really his mornings, and so consequently his best time.

Lymhal dragged himself out of bed and began a search for his clothes.

***

"Now remember," bellowed the instructor. "Try and keep together those of you who are new. Don't leave other's straggling. I want you to try and encourage each other around the course. Go down to the bottom of the estate and follow the track round to the back of the manor. Remember don't overdo it. Jog a little, then rest a while and so on. The fitter ones of you can go at your own pace – but remember, if you experience any pain or breathlessness, then slow down, walk it off. For those of you who are new this week don't worry if it takes a little longer to get round, you can't get lost, especially if you stick together."

The instructor checked his watch. "Right then, off you go."

The small knot of people huddled together on the grass outside looked around uncertainly at the driveway wending its way out of sight in the early morning mist, and then reluctantly moved off at an extremely slow trot.

Lymhal was disappointed. He had hoped there would be some younger people like himself holidaying at the farm but the majority of Hadleigh's clients were middle-aged business men or wealthy ladies with nothing better to do with their time. He felt acutely embarrassed taking up a lazy lope after the group of plump individuals wobbling off down the drive.

It was cold at this time of the morning and it made him yearn for the comfort of his bed, but now that he was awake he decided to show old Mayhew just how fit he was. He passed the group, ignoring the instructor's advice and sped on along the driveway until he reached the wrought alloy gates of the manor's inner lawns. He soon found the track the instructor had meant them to follow and trotted along until it passed through some sparse woodland. He climbed a slight rise and jogged to a halt to catch his breath.

It was a long time since he'd done any running and his body felt hot and shaken. To add to his fatigue he was lacking his normal quota of sleep, as he had lain awake to well past three o'clock that morning and he felt abnormally light-headed and queasy. He yawned and pushed himself on, reaching the edge of the copse minutes later. At this rate, he realised he'd be back at the manor sooner than expected.

He stood on some higher ground and searched to his left for the group of runners still behind him. They had already stopped and most were walking. Still breathing heavily, Lymhal looked around at the soft ferns of the woodland and considered trying to snatch a half-hour's kip amongst them.

He would tell the instructor he got carried away and ran right the way round the grounds.

But the ferns were still wet with the early morning dew and although the undergrowth was thick in places and the sun was quickly warming the land, he knew the strangeness of the woods would prevent any form of sleep.

What he wanted was some form of shelter.

He found it on the edge of the woodland, a ramshackle old barn, still full of the previous year's straw. Lymhal found an entrance and squeezed inside. Some dry bales and mounds of hay looked warm and inviting. He climbed up to the top of one mound and crawled into a tiny alcove under the rafters. He'd never slept in straw before, the thought excited him.

He curled into the foetal position and closed his eyes.

The straw heated quickly beneath him, exuding a moist warmth. Lymhal nestled deeper into the stack, his track suit insulating him against any drafts.

Within minutes he was asleep.

"Looking for Cherry?" a voice asked. "She's over there."

"Need a hand?"

"Help him, someone!"

Lymhal woke fleetingly. He knew he was hovering between sleep and consciousness and that his alien environment wasn't conducive to the type of sleep he needed. He nuzzled deeper into the straw, the thought that he had plenty of time before he was due back further relaxing him.

"Come on then, come on."

"He's not here really, Cherry!"

"Cherry!"

"Cherry!"

"Cherry," Lymhal moaned.

She stood before him, decked in a Victorian style dress, her hair tied back with a ribbon. The vision was hazy, obfuscated. Lymhal sought clarity.

"Thought I'd take you to London," she was saying. "See the sights, duck'ee," and she smirked at her own humour.

For some reason Lymhal was afraid. He didn't want to go. He couldn't be sure what of or why, but he shook his head irritably in his sleep.

Her hand in his…

Warmth, light. An open expanse.

Her words. "This better then?" Chiding? Resentful?

Lymhal could see her more clearly now, was viewing her from behind, side on, almost a profile. Her cheeks were round and full. Her eyes stared. Her hair was still swept back, tumbling around her neck. Far away a door was banging. A cool breeze brushed his face. She felt it too.

"It's breaking in: You're weak."

Lymhal shifted in the straw.

"Didn't he like London?"

"There's lots to see in London!"

"Never go to London."

"You're going. I'll see you tomorrow."

"Wait..!" Lymhal tried to say but found himself awake.

When he arrived back he was late. He tried to explain that he'd got lost but the instructor seemed to have already lost interest in him.

"Been sleeping in that old barn, more likely," grunted an old gentleman over breakfast.

***

That evening Lymhal was grateful of an early bedtime. The exercise in the morning and a long walk in the afternoon had left him exhausted and by nine he had retired to his room to rest. Scattered about were rough sketches and drawings of Cherry as he'd seen her that morning, executed at odd moments; the Victorian dress; embroidery and sequins and several sketches of her face from various angles. Now he sat at his desk, his head in one hand the other laying limp in his lap, viewing the assorted pictures.

"Girlfriend," a voice asked?

Startled, Lymhal looked round to find an attractive woman leaning over him. She was his neighbour from a few doors down – a cupboard and a storeroom separating their rooms. Normally he would have been more receptive, but tonight he was too tired to take advantage of her forwardness.

"No, not really. I keep seeing her in my dreams."

"Lucky boy. She's very pretty."

"Persistent too."

"You mean she occurs regularly?"

"Almost every day."

"You should have a word with Professor Gaskin. I believe he dabbled in oneiromancy"

"On – erio – what?"

"Oneiromancy – the interpretation of dreams.

"Oh! Thanks, I will."

Intrigued by this, Lymhal chose that very same evening to seek out Professor Gaskin, finding him in one of the TV lounges.

"Er, Mr. Gaskin...?" The old professor was nearly asleep himself.

"Eh? Oh, hello my boy. Off to bed?"

"Um, no…I've been having some rather vivid and persistent dreams lately and I wondered if you might like to hear about them?

"Delighted. Fire away."

Lymhal recited as many meetings with Cherry as he could remember, keeping them roughly in chronological order.

"Interesting," murmured the professor at last. "Very interesting. You say all of the dreams run in a sort of order, like a normal conversation?"

"Yes, it's as if she really exists on another plane."

"Hm, you see dreams are the direct result of the subconscious amusing itself. You're sure you're not harboring any pent-up emotions over a girl or anything like that?"

Lymhal shook his head emphatically. "No. Not at all. That's what makes it so strange."

"Well, as long as they are not frightening, I wouldn't worry. It'll probably blow over."

"You don't think I need to see a psychoanalyst or anything?"

"Good God, no! Enjoy them while they last."

***

He was standing in an expanse of sparse vegetation. It stretched forever before him. The plants were bulbous, fleshy things with just a few frond-like structures sprouting from the tops. The ground on which he was standing comprised of white and beige sand and rock. Cherry was standing nearby. He had slept deeply that night, the fresh air of the day almost knocking him out. Outside his window the birds were re-establishing their territory as the light crept over the land. The dream was vivid, solid and clear, and he was in complete control of his faculties.

He walked over to join her.

"Where are we," he asked?

She shrugged.

Lymhal felt an irritation rise within him. He shuffled round and stood before her staring rudely into her face. At his own leisure he inspected every detail. Her skin was perfect, unblemished. There was nothing striking about her eyes, he found, they were just a plain watery blue; only the shaggy unkempt style of her hair emphasised them.

But overall she was remarkably pretty.

Lymhal stood back and admired her.

She stared back coldly.

She was wearing only a bikini top and tight-fitting shorts and her feet were bare on the sandy rock. Lymhal nodded to himself agreeably. He was feeling decidedly cocky and arrogant and considered stretching out and cupping her pert breasts in his hands, but thought that might be pushing things a bit too far. He crossed his arms and laughed at her.

"What's so funny?"

Lymhal caught his breath.

"You."

"Oh?" She shifted her weight.

"Why do you keep appearing in my dreams," he shouted?

He hadn't meant to rant, but a capriciousness had spawned it.

"I want you," she averred, reaching out to him, sliding her hands up his chest.

"You do?"

She smiled, squinting in the sun.

"Why?"

Cherry looked away, almost shrugging again.

Lymhal searched her face, found a guilt there.

What was it?

Why him?

He moved to her, clasping her tapering back, feeling a light cotton beneath his fingers.

A turquoise T-shirt was now covering her breasts.

Lymhal worked his fingers up underneath to feel her skin. She shivered.

"You're cold."

She nodded.

"Take me somewhere," he said, pulling her to him, holding her close.

"Where?"

Lymhal thought for a moment. "A party," he exclaimed! "Up the road from where I live there's a bowling rink, high up over the sports complex. It's got a fantastic view out over the beach and ocean and the main balcony is really futuristic. Make one there."

"Alright."

Lymhal sat in his favourite place, on a padded seat near the beginning of the balcony. From here he could look out over the ocean and also keep his eye on the small floor that was often cleared for dancing.

His friends were all around him. A party was in session.

Lymhal asked who's it was, but his friends just laughed and shrugged. They'd obviously gate-crashed it. "Hey!" he suddenly blurted. "Where's Cherry?"

"Who?"

"Cherry, my new girl. Wait till you see her!" Elated, Lymhal jumped down from his seat and made quite a commotion staggering about the rink shouting for her. He'd obviously had too much to drink. Damn it, trust him to think of something else and lose the thread just when he wanted her.

Other girls sidled up to him, sharing their drinks but Lymhal stared past them in search of Cherry. He stumbled about, panicking, pushing aside hazy visions.

Then he saw her.

She was attired in a pinafore dress and roller skates of a bygone age, skating around the rink to join him. He realised then, looking around that others were in fancy dress. He too had a hat on with an immense feather sprouting from it but sensed he'd cadged it off someone else to mingle with the occasion.

Cherry twirled to a stop before him.

She looked fantastic, he mused in his inebriated way, and resolved to run his hands up her lovely legs just as soon as they could be alone. "Come meet the gang," he shouted.

He was the envy of the party. His friends crowded around. She sat in his lap, her legs across his. He was catching the sidelong glances of other girls as they eyed his new consort. She certainly was pretty.

"Good party," she asked?

"Brilliant!"

He let his hand fall casually onto her thigh, feeling the firm muscle through the fishnet stockings. The band struck up with his favourite song and the words drifted over the laughter, the hubbub of the guests. Cherry was grinning sheepishly. She pulled his hand from her leg and placed it in her lap. Lymhal felt a passion ignite within him. He slid his hand to the inside of her thighs, kissing her fully.

Something was happening. They broke from the embrace. Lymhal felt a fury rising inside him.

No don't! Not now!

They were on their feet. He relaxed. He realised they were slipping away from the party; all was well.

As they neared the exit, Lymhal clasped Cherry's buttocks. He could hardly wait.

She turned, they embraced.

Warm lips, a hint of perfume; a nuance of lipstick.

Lymhal floated, his soul melted.

A hand on his shoulder, rough, unruly. An angry face. A boyfriend? Impossible.

"What's up?"

"Beat it!"

Another tug.

"It's outside!" She lashed out with her fist. The boy tried a cuff. Lymhal disengaged himself and felt everyone turning to him.

Shouts of encouragement. His friends. He had lots of friends. He ripped the hand away that groped for his jacket, reached out himself for purchase and drew back his fist.

Events were slowing. It wasn't fair. The blow was parried. Some other force was intervening, hampering him. His wrists were seized. Cherry was nowhere to be seen. The party was dissolving. Enraged, Lymhal swung out blindly. "Bastard!" he screamed. "I'll kill you! I'll kill you!"

A sharp slap brought him to his senses. Lymhal realised he had the matron in a vicious grip and relinquished his hold.

An orderly who had heard the ruckus appeared in the doorway.

"You're awake now, I see," said the matron, trying to straighten her uniform.

"Yes," replied Lymhal, stammering. "I'm – I'm sorry; I…

"If this goes on, my boy, you'd better see a doctor," and she swirled out of the room.

Lymhal sat forward and ran a hand over his face. He realised he was trembling. The wrench had been tremendous.

He sighed and cupped his head in his hands.

***

"And you say you've been having these dreams almost daily. Do they recur or are they a variation of the same dream?"

"It's not the variant of any one dream doc'. It's a continuous sequence of events with this one particular girl. She's so persistent, and what's more they're so vivid and real. It's as if I'm living two lives. One in the present and one in my dreams." Lymhal sighed and leaned back in his chair.

On the matron's insistence he had gone to see Hadleigh's resident physician in his tiny surgery.

He was beginning to feel the definite need for some expert medical advice, and there was something else that he hadn't realised before, he was becoming frightened.

But if Lymhal expected Doctor Baines to accept such a challenge as a break from the tedium of the farm's normal cases, he was sorely disappointed. The GP simply fobbed him off with some sleeping pills and sent him on his way. Lymhal stuffed the container into a pocket and forgot about them. If anything, he needed something to wake him up, not knock him out, as the matron could verify. He decided to seek out Professor Gaskin again.

"I suppose you heard about this morning," he remarked once he'd found the academic and seated himself across from him.

"I did," chuckled the old man. "Seems you nearly gave the matron a black eye. Some dream."

"It was."

"Care to tell me about it?"

Lymhal recounted his experiences.

"Strange. Very strange," murmured Professor Gaskin after the account. "…and intriguing. Don't you have any other sort of dream, you know, about normal things?"

Lymhal shook his head despondently.

"She dominates them all, even naps?"

The professor nodded.

"You aren't taking drugs for anything are you," he asked suddenly, leaning forward in his chair and eyeing Lymhal suspiciously? "For any condition or other, a bang on the head perhaps?"

"No," he answered, wondering what the professor had in mind.

"Have you been under any treatment lately, for depression or anything like that?"

"No," he laughed.

"Hmm."

The professor leaned back and seemed to study Lymhal for a moment.

"Do you drink much, Lymhal," he asked? "Alcohol," and he gestured with his hand, clearing up any misinterpretation?

"Only weekends really," he replied sincerely. "I tend to have a few with friends then, but in the week it's usually soft drinks."

"None since you've come here."

"No, I didn't know the place had a bar."

Professor Gaskin chuckled and seemed to relax. He glanced at his wristwatch and realised it was time for his tablets.

"We'll have to continue this another time, Lymhal, if that's alright?"

"Of course."

"I'll tell you what. When will you be sleeping next?"

Lymhal shrugged. I don't feel up to much today. I may take a nap later in the afternoon."

"Good. Well, if you do and you dream of this girl again, come and see me. I'd like to take some notes."

"Thanks Mr. Gaskin," and Lymhal rose to help the old man out of his chair; "I'm glad someone's taking an interest."

Lymhal excused himself from the activities that day, feigning a headache. He spent the rest of the morning in his room sketching, and after lunch ambled through the stately gardens of the manor. At times he found he actually had to take a rest upon one of the many bench seats provided. This lassitude bothered him and he wondered if the sudden change in the air was beginning to affect him. He had, after all, never spent a day outside his own town for years and the fresh air of the countryside really could be soporific if you were not used to it. He stretched out on the seat and yawned lazily.

"Beautiful isn't it?"

"Mm..."

Cherry nuzzled deeper into the side of his chest. It was still a warm, sunny afternoon but the shade of the trees around the seat made their little arbour cool and refreshing.

A rabbit hopped from a hedgerow to where she had thrown some nuts and Lymhal noticed a squirrel scampering down from an old oak tree to gain his share.

Songbirds twittered and as a leitmotiv bullfrogs croaked in a pond nearby.

"Do you do this," he asked, enjoying the sounds?

"No. It's here all the time, for you to find."

"I'm asleep, aren't I?"

Cherry remained silent.

Lymhal drummed his fingers in a single cadence and sighed.

Was he going to spend the rest of his life asleep?

He disengaged himself from Cherry and sat forward, studying his hands. He remembered the party and his amorous, almost lecherous intentions, but now his mood had changed.

"Tell me," he said. "Am I going mad?"

"No, you're not mad. It's me who's mad."

She stood up, scattering the animals. Lymhal contemplating that last remark, looked on.

The dark blue denim jeans she was wearing hugged her curvy hips, and a heavy cable pullover highlighted her femininity by falling in a tantalising curve over them.

'This is real', he thought. *'But it can't be; I'm asleep!'*

The crack made Cherry jump. His surroundings vibrated, jerked.

Lymhal looked down at his stinging hands and insisted; "I'm dreaming."

"I'm dreaming," he repeated out loud, standing!

He considered doing something violent or stupid, like trying to climb a tree or fly perhaps, but the tomfoolery left him as soon as it had come. He realised his hands were still smarting, and sighed, sitting back down.

Perhaps if he assumed his former position?

He lay back down on the seat.

After a moment, he wasn't sure if he was awake or asleep!

"Christ," he shouted, jumping up! "This is beginning to get to me." He put his hands on his hips and stared wildly around at the flora.

"I'm going flying," he told no one in particular.

Nothing happened.

"Alright." Lymhal marched from the arbour and through the gardens to a patio at the back of the manor. He mounted the stone steps two at a time, climbed onto the balustrade, and leapt off.

Lymhal hit the ground with a sickening thud.

It was all the more sickening for him. At the last second he had realised it wasn't going to work and he tried to correct his swallow dive into the grass, with the result that one knee had been punched up into his mouth and his left wrist allowed to break most of the fall.

It did indeed prove one thing as he woke, flying was for the birds, even in his dreams.

He'd fallen off the bench, or so it seemed, rolled in his sleep, but as he staggered to his feet something made his blood freeze.

***

He sat in the surgery, daubing at a swollen lip. His bottom teeth were a little loose but the nurse didn't think he needed to see a dentist. She bandaged his sprained wrist and sent him packing with yet another micro-container of pills. Lymhal jammed them into his pocket and weaved off in search of the bar.

***

Professor Gaskin sat in his room. Then, in one decisive movement he got to his feet and stood before a section of books. Since he had retired and taken up permanent residence at Hadliegh in his senior years, the academic's library which had adorned the walls of his house had been thinned out and condensed to fit into the two rooms he now occupied. Widowed, alone, and dependant on Hadleigh's amenities due to an abnormal form of sclerosis eating away at his legs, he stood, not contemplating his own predicament but that of young Lymhal Morey's. His fingers moved along the shelf, noting the titles as he did so. He still had several volumes on 'This thing called Sleep' Thinski; a volume on early oneiromancy and its various origins; a concise history of the subject; and various old tomes on para-sciences that had once been respected as viable theses but had since been crushed under the wheels of modern revelations; and as a respected and valid work he still had an old copy of Freud's Interpretation of Dreams. But without reading a passage the professor knew the mysteries of sleep still remained inconclusive.

The rest was just conjecture.

He sighed and shuffled over to the window, wondering if there was anything in Lymhal's medical file that would help.

Hadleigh's small surgery was quiet and empty when the professor ambled into the reception. He was more than relieved to find Dr Baines out and his secretary at a computer terminal behind a glass-panelled dispensary. He smiled to himself. He got on with Baines' secretary.

He tapped on the window and, after making sure she knew who it was, let himself in.

"Hello, Professor Gaskin. Have you come for your prescription?"

"Er, no. Actually I'm doing a little research," he whispered conspiratorially, "and wondered if I could have a look at Lymhal Morey's file?"

The secretary looked puzzled for a moment but then smiled warmly. She understood how it must be for a man so active in his former life to find himself with time on his hands. She understood too that he had considerable medical expertise in his younger days and although Dr. Baines was usually cold to any of his suggestions, she knew that if the professor could help anyone in any way, he would.

"Help yourself professor," she replied. "I'll put the kettle on."

Once he'd found the file, the professor wasn't surprised to find that Lymhal had been given a clean bill of health by Hadleigh's resident physician, and was cited A-1 with regard to his physical fitness. He had no childhood diseases such as Chorea or Diphtheria, and had no abnormalities like autism listed. He had been sensible enough to keep off the drugs and atomisers so rife among the young a few years ago, and he wasn't being prescribed any medicines, nor had he just come off any, erasing a possible rebound effect so common with suppressants.

His genetic heredity was clear, and Lymhal had certainly never had any cause to see a psychiatrist of any kind – something that hardly surprised Professor Gaskin.

Staring at the file, the professor backtracked further and whisked over any physiological upsets he might have missed. Diet for instance. There was absolute proof that almost everyone was allergic in some way to one of the thousands of food products readily available, and of course the allergy often affected the patient's sleeping patterns. Could be something there, he mused, the sudden change to the farm's natural foodstuffs. He made a mental note to ask. The change in the environment too was something to be considered.

All in all Professor Gaskin's line of thought led him to conclude that Lymhal was no schizophrenic, nor – in his opinion – was he suffering from any form of neurosis which confirmed his earlier assumption; Lymhal was no heretic lapsing into flights of fancy.

"Lymhal Morey," stated the secretary in a question? She had just re-entered the small office with a tray. "You know, I'm sure that's the young lad that we just had in here not so long ago."

"Oh?"

"Yes. Had a nasty fall apparently. Yes, here it is. I haven't had a chance to enter the details yet. Sprained wrist and bruised jawbone. What do you –"

"Professor. Professor Gaskin..?" But the professor had already disappeared out of the surgery.

When the professor found him, Lymhal was not only worse for wear, but worse for drink too. The eminent academic managed to coax him out of the clubroom and back to his own where he was seated, and presently a black coffee placed steaming in front of him.

"You've had a few drinks," observed the professor, somewhat unnecessarily?

"It's the weekend," responded Lymhal.

The professor chuckled and drew up a seat opposite.

Lymhal remembered his manners too late and the old professor was seated before he could rise.

"I assume," said Professor Gaskin, "that you've had another encounter with this girl?"

Lymhal nodded.

"Care to tell me about it?"

Bored, he began to describe his latest meeting with Cherry.

At the end of it he produced a folded ladies handkerchief, now covered in blood.

The professor took it and fondled it as if it was the first piece of tangible evidence Lymhal had produced.

There was nothing extraordinary about the square piece of cloth, Lymhal knew. It could have been dropped by any one of the ladies sauntering through the gardens, but he and the professor considered it very unlikely that his injuries could have come from simply rolling off a bench.

The professor took a ruminative intake of breath and placed the handkerchief on the small coffee table in front of them.

Lymhal was beginning to wonder if at last the professor was thinking him a crackpot or attention seeker.

"And there's no medical history of dementia or blackouts in your family?"

Lymhal shook his head.

The professor leaned forward in his chair and pinched his lower lip thoughtfully. The lad before him was either a brilliant liar, or in some real danger of hurting himself – if someone didn't get to the bottom of this. In fact, in the light of this recent incident it might be wise to advise Lymhal to see a psychiatrist; for it seemed to him that that the boy was definitely hallucinating or worse suffering from some new kind of fugue. He decided to run over the details one more time.

"Let's go back to the start," persisted the professor. "Can you remember the first time this girl appeared in your dreams?"

Lymhal thought for a moment, but then he shook his head again in frustration. "No, but it was several weeks ago now, and she's been fairly persistent ever since."

"You can, you know, learn to control your dreams to a point. Have you ever tried that?"

"Yes," said Lymhal, "often, but she always outwits me."

And so it went on. Yes, his life was fairly sedentary, and yes, he could do with a little more exercise, although he never felt the need for it. And yes, Lymhal had girlfriends and a fairly fulfilling and varied sex life with several of his consorts. No, he didn't know that dreams often compensated for one thing or another, but it was the matron's intervention that morning that had evoked the incident. No, he didn't remember any symbolic connotations in his dreams with Cherry, she dominated them all.

Hoping it would help, Lymhal backtracked still further and filled in about his schooldays and his adolescence.

By the time they had finished, Lymhal could see the old professor was tired. He fervently hoped there had been something he could pick up on or expose or extirpate, because he hadn't been wrong about the strange feeling of nausea in the pit of his stomach when he left the surgery that morning, the feeling of an animal cornered and frightened.

The professor was shaking his head, even as he stared at him. Lymhal began to wonder if the eminent oneirocritic had exhausted the wealth of his knowledge.

Sensing the session was at an end, he rose wearily, and after assuring the professor he was feeling alright, bid him an early good night.

He left Gaskin's room and weaved unsteadily towards his own.

Lymhal sat at his desk, staring at the picture.

She was, he realised, beautiful.

It was late. He had worked incessantly on the drawing, employing pastels and inks and later sealing the colours with a lacquer: A full portrait, over three feet in height. The foreground was one of his own design but the backdrop and her immediate surroundings were of the arbour they had sat in that afternoon, the animals around her, the squirrel and the rabbits and birds in the trees. He had come to know her so well that any one of her countenances were easy for him, and Lymhal had chosen a soft far away smile as she gazed down at a rabbit near her feet. No bows or frills. He'd drawn her in the cable pullover and tight jeans of that afternoon, feeling the casual apparel emphasised her well-proportioned body. The rock she sat on gave a nice back-dropping contrast of grey and black and he had taken full opportunity when outlining the curves of her hip and thigh, the delicate ankles.

The overall pose had pleased him, hunched ever so slightly, legs straight out as she sat perched against a boulder, her hands tucked down between them as she took delight in the animals surrounding her. An almost angelic pose but one offset by the fashion of her clothes.

In her face however, was the true artistry, embodying every hue to bring out her full beauty, the pastels being ideal for defining a perfectly clear skin. Her face shone as if it had an inner radiance, the picture itself exhibiting an almost three-dimensional quality, the true mark of genius, Lymhal recognised.

He was exhausted, having kept a rapt pose for hours.

He washed and undressed and after a while slipped into bed. He tried to evoke Cherry. He wanted an opinion, but more importantly, he wanted her.

An hour passed and although he was tired, sleep eluded him. He tossed and turned and eventually remembered the sleeping pills the doctor had given him.

It was against his better judgement but his teeth were hurting and his wrist ached, and he slipped out of bed to rummage in his jacket hanging on the back of the door.

The tiny pills looked ridiculously small and impotent.

Lymhal tipped three into the palm of his hand and after a moment's contemplation, washed them down and curled up back under the sheets.

They're not going to work, he realised, then, almost as quickly, he knew they had. He felt an excitement ignite within, an uncontrollable yearning.

He turned. Cherry was sitting on the edge of the bed beside him, admiring his work.

He reached out and touched her. She was solid, real. His fingertips brushed a scant negligee and slid round to caress the softness of her belly.

"Any good," he whispered?

She seemed absorbed in the picture.

"It's beautiful."

Lymhal put his arms around her waist experiencing her warmth, pulling her to him. "I wish I could be asleep all the time," he murmured as she slid into his bed.

***

Professor Gaskin stood in the bedroom and stared at the portrait. To his untrained eye it was magnificent. Lymhal certainly had talent – and the young lady, she certainly was pretty. "What imagina –" he caught himself saying.

Confused he turned and looked down at Lymhal.

Matron had found him comatose early that morning. She'd given up trying to wake him and gone about her business. At eleven, having not seen or heard of him, she returned to his room to check on him.

Ten minutes later, she was convinced something was wrong.

She had hurried to fetch Dr Baines and inform Mr Mayhew. Now an ambulance was on its way to Hedliegh to pick him up.

Gaskin's professional bearing had never elicited the respect and comradeship he had hoped from the resident physician but he had no need of his medical skills to recognise the symptoms of a coma.

There was still the hint of a strange perfume in the room and a cold abject horror slid down the professor's back as he bent to touch a diaphanous negligee left lying on the bed.

***

Lymhal was in Paris. He'd been in love with the city ever since he'd visited as a boy on his school holidays. He had picked it and in a flash they were there. With its quaint little cafes and avenues, protected from industrialisation, Paris was the place to be when you were in love. But as he strolled arm in arm with Cherry through the streets, he had a vague sensation that people were shouting at him, calling to him to, *"Go back! Go back!"*

Lymhal wondered what it all meant.

Arm in arm he and Cherry walked on.

In a high wire compound people danced with apes and baboons. Blue statues of Olympian gods atop a theatre were coming to life and leaving their pedestals. He was being accosted by various colleens who handed him pictures of Cherry as a baby, remarking on her wispy blonde curls. Lymhal smiled placatingly. A crowd crossed the road and engulfed them. He saw on their faces deceit, smarmy histrionics, even though they were smiling and congratulating them both. He felt compelled to laugh, to join in, even as he was jostled. Then, amongst the crowd, he felt a wrench, a tear in the fabric of his soul. A terrible sadness welled up inside. He called for Cherry but knew she was gone, had given him the slip. Tears welled in his eyes. *"Cherry!"* he called, stumbling on. *"Cherry!"*

Meanwhile, Cherry passed through the gate.

On the following day, at exactly twelve minutes past midday, all electrical activity in Lymhal's brain had ceased for more than four hours and he was cited clinically dead. After a grief-filled decision, and against everything Professor Gaskin could do, Lymhal was switched off.

At that very moment Mrs Berry in the maternity ward gave birth to a bouncing seven-pound baby girl. Everybody commented on her wispy blonde curls.

***

The End

Life's a Champagne Bubble

First published in *Butterflies and Bloomers's Magazine* July 1986 – M Gillian

Life is a Champagne Bubble; Text @ copyright Christopher E. Howard 1986.

Reprinted 1988, 1989, 1990; 1993, 1994, 1995, 1997, 1998,

2001, 2002, 2005, 2009, 2015, 2022

Author's note; 'Life is a Champagne Bubble' is one of those little pieces of writing that has gone on through the years – not exactly earning me loads of money but on the other hand keeping my enthusiasm up when other rejections loom, and generally greeting me like an old friend whenever another editor decides to air it.

It's been reprinted so many times I've virtually lost count but at one stage it was being reprinted in various magazines, pamphlets and collections almost every year!

This small piece of writing is indicative of what's become known in the world of literature as the 'Short-short' – the fabled 'ten-minute-read'. Popular years ago with the 'fanzine and pamphlet era' it died out for some time as the 'trade-paperback' took centre stage.

With the introduction of Indie-publishing and the e-book revolution the shorter written stories have been making quite a comeback – our lives becoming that much more hectic, coupled with the versatility of the phone, tablet, or Kindle means one can access almost any media at any time...and so the 'ten-minute-read' has once again graced our lives – and long may it live!

So here it is yet again for your enjoyment.

Life is a Champagne Bubble

'Life's a Champagne Bubble' Text ©copyright C.E.Howard 1986

First appearance in Butterflies and Bloomer's – M. Gillian

Their eyes met across the translucent floor, and as if by gravity they were drawn together. He was rotund and handsome, she petite and demure. They circled slowly, each appraising the other's curves.

Around them the party was in full fizz, couples rising in ascendance, singles bobbing to the beat, all locked in a heady fanfare of gaiety and emotions; for in this frenzied free-for-all lovers were destined to meet, fall in love and procreate, ensuring the survival of their creed.

Time was short but not so short as to divest of etiquette and forget one's manners. No. The clan of Moët and Chandon reached far back into history and were cultured and proud: Inherent instincts to these two champions of the effervescent world.

Already they had attracted the attention of some of the onlookers. In suave fashion he reached out to her, employing reverent deference, genuflecting before proffering the engagement to twirl.

Twittering coyly, she acquiesced, slipping delicately and nimbly into his airstream. At first he was too dazzled by her beauty to do more than a light eddying quickstep. The way the light gleamed off her, irradiated her, shone from her to almost blind him.

She was truly a bubble to behold!

She too found his stature alluring. He was so big and strong, he had his own centre of gravity, a nebulous cluster of sparkling liquid and gas that gleamed at her from inside with a thousand twinkling suns. So thick and hard was his skin, the light imbued him with a magnificent matt finish.

By Cork! She was the envy of all here.

He saluted her again, dipping around her in the currents, seemingly reading the compliments in her countenance, accepting them with courtesy.

She let herself be taken, releasing her energies as they slipped into a glissading waltz.

The floor began to descend as they rose in the panoply of dancers. Yet they held the centre of the party, finding their own vacuum, having room for nobody but each other. Those around began to applaud, to fizzle out, watch the show and make room for these two rising stars.

He took them into a breath-taking spin, holding her close, enjoying the exhilaration of the move, then smoothed out to execute the tango.

She surrendered to him, accompanying his every move, spinning here, pivoting there, receiving commendations with every innovation.

She was the bell of the ball.

The atmosphere intensified, pressures built upon pressure as they swirled around their own nucleus, jiving, rock n' rolling, doing the twist. He was lost to the moment. The samba and rumba followed; the crowd cheering them on, daring them to meld. And touch they must, for they were made for each other, a match made in the glittering heavens.

Far above the dance floor now a new fervency gripped them, driven by the potent ambience. Others fell away, the light dimming, concentrating on their central space. Their rolling slowed, the tension between them mounting, knowing no bounds. She capitulated, pervading his skin, welcoming him. The magic surged, crescendoing.

He surrendered, exploding.

Their atoms mingled, energies fusing, hearts expanding, skin bursting in a scintillating shower of bejewelled droplets, each tiny protoplasm of new-born energy.

The shower rained down on the party, on the couples, singles and dancers alike!

The End

***

Comment by one editor that I really liked;

(I was exhausted after reading this – a sort of,

'out of the dictionary and onto the dance floor episode'.

Quite exhilarating really, with images of Torville and Dean

dancing to Ravel's 'Bolero, or something like that!

Thanks Chris!)

Starlove

'Starlove' Text ©copyright C.E.Howard 1990
First appearance Dream magazine – Trevor Jones.

At the sound of the five o'clock klaxon, Louis Barns threw down his file and walked to the factory washroom. There, among fifty to sixty other jostling workmen he struggled out of his overalls and fought his way to the sinks to wash his hands.

The end of a working week: The evening held no prospects for him. At twenty-eight Louis was beginning to feel the normal aspects of life – courtship; marriage; a place of his own – starting to pass him by. Short, overweight, and lacking in any cosmetic quality, he possessed not even the drive to achieve the normal things in life.

His hands only marginally cleaner, he wiped them on the towels provided and went to stand in line by the timekeeper.

Endomorphy was to blame he realised, leaving the factory to begin his lonely walk home. The ennui and longueurs that had plagued him from his school days were a direct result of his physical inability, the listlessness inherent with his roundness he guessed. He lived, or simply existed for the pleasures of a comfortable home life; his bedroom's extensive entertainment centre; and his one other avocation – his place at the bar of the 'Spacehopper' not five minutes' walk from his home.

He climbed out of the dell in which his and other factories were clustered, turned left along the flower beds of Protile Industries and engaged the path that ran around the storage area of the spaceport.

There was someone new on tonight, he noticed, passing through a heavy turnstile affair but he gave the uniformed figure in the security box a friendly wave anyway, which probably saved him from having to identify himself.

Normally he would have cut straight across the spaceport, keeping to the narrow roadway, but tonight something compelled him to walk around the perimeter fence.

Here sometimes there were things of interest to see; stockpiles of spare parts for the cargo freighters; rocket motors; freshly painted and emblazoned fuel tanks for the deep space liners; the latest weaponry attachments; sometimes a complete replacement cockpit or tail fin for one of the mighty shuttles, all awaiting their destinations. Tonight however, Louis was disappointed. Many of the plots between the warehouses were empty. A large object further in looked interesting but it was swathed in dense polythene that had gone all but opaque with condensation.

Irritated by the premonition that had proved fruitless, he quickened his pace and strove to make up for lost time.

In doing so he very nearly missed a small collection of crates and machinery squeezed in between a row of tin sheds.

Louis stopped and backtracked.

It was mostly spare parts for specialised tools, due for a new colony world somewhere far out from the colonial hub, intriguing but beyond Louis by light years, but what did arrest his attention and was far more promising was a long metal box standing amongst some other taller equipment set against one shack. Over a metre high and more than three long with one huge section of glass, it had to be a cage. Louis had heard of livestock being dumped out here before, there being nowhere else for it to go, but apart from some iridescent blobs of jelly and some other rat-like creatures he'd been unlucky. He picked his way over the pallets of machinery to take a peek inside.

His eyes rested immediately on a large brown bundle huddled in one corner.

Purple skin showed through a thick chestnut fur. Long slender arms wrapped tightly around short stubby legs.

It looked to Louis like an ape, or other such primate he had seen in zoos but its large triangulated ears and unusual colouring gave it a pronounced alien element. Even as he looked he knew it was not crouched in that one corner for warmth. The cage was heated, kept at a constant thirty-two degrees centigrade according to the thermometer, and the lights of a display panel belied any malfunction. No, the animal was sitting in a way that almost advertised its inactivity. The creature was lonely.

Louis studied its environment. The oblong box was cut into two compartments the aft section a cosy straw-filled den into which the animal obviously crawled at night. The dissecting wall was festooned with simplified panels adorned with all sorts of levers, switches and buttons; the animal obviously expressed an intelligence.

In the centre of living quarters a small geodesic framework rested on which the animal was supposed to perform light callisthenics. Strange brightly coloured objects were strewn about the floor; Toys, Louis inferred, yet despite these and other playthings it was plain to see the creature was unhappy. He pressed his fingers against the thick slab of plastiglass.

Would the animal respond if he tapped it?

Tentatively, Louis tried.

His fingertips sounded dull and flat against the dense plastic, but slowly the head lifted, swivelling to discover the source of the cadence.

He tapped again, eager now to gaze upon this creature from the stars.

The animal blinked, focused, and found Louis.

He froze in mid-movement. Louis was astonished. The creature was beautiful. No, beautiful was the wrong word. Aesthetics had played a part here, battling with its simian ancestry and winning but it was still an ape; its hunched body asymmetrical. Captivating.

Yes, he thought. That was it. The animal was captivating. A strangely feline head housed two enormous eyes that extended to a point somewhere over the temples. There were no irises that Louis could discern, the sclera were simply two bulbous pear drops curving round to meet above a delicately flared pair of nostrils. A filmy lid encompassed the eye, folding back into the brow.

Every blink seemed a slow calculated movement.

Louis pressed his palm against the glass, and, evoking no response, tapped lightly again with his fingertips.

The animal rose, standing.

He wondered what sex it might be. Its arms and torso were sinewy and graceful suggestive of femininity, but its feet were large and unattractive and its hands had long sturdy fingers, capable, Louis guessed, of some strength. It was shorter than he had at first supposed, comparing its slender arms to its muscular yet stockier legs, and definitely simian in its overall appearance, but its eyes held an uncanny mesmerising lustre that Louis had never seen before in an animal.

He found a box among the crates around him and arranged it to sit on. The creature was bored; Louis would sit with it for a while.

Long pyriform eyes stared into dark brown.

Louis felt a twinge of unease. What could he do now that he had attracted its attention? He desperately didn't want to disappoint it.

He rummaged in his satchel and produced his thermos flask, a bulky tube of silver-blue with various buttons and dials aligned across an inset. The animal stared attentively at Louis, as – activating selected controls – he poured first a small cool orange drink; then a warm, sweetened beverage of chocolate and coffee – a peculiarity of his own taste; and then finally, a fizzy mauve cola mixture.

The creature cocked its head from side to side as it puzzled over the colourful concoctions and the fact that they all poured from the same vessel, one giving off a slight evanescing spiral of steam in the late afternoon air. Louis arranged the cups and flask on the ground in front of the glass and sorted through his bag for other items of intrigue.

To his delight he discovered an old pen-torch at the bottom, dusty and rusted, and after wiping it clean, held it between his fingers, playing with the beam. Amusement showed on the animal's face and it wrung its hands together as it shuffled up to the glass.

Louis smiled. What else did he have to offer?

He emptied the satchel out onto the ground and sifted over old pieces of metal and micro-switches that had followed him home. One or two of the items glinted in the early evening floodlights of the spaceport and he singled them out, flicking them toward the glass for the ape's closer inspection.

At long last Louis had exhausted his supply of gadgets and trumperies and he began to place them all back into his bag. He would have liked to drop the pen-torch into the animal's cage, but without even looking Louis knew the vents would balk, even the permeation of harmful gases or fumes, never mind a solid object.

For a while he just stared at the creature through the thick sheet of plastiglass, then he waggled his fingers in a cheery goodbye and was gone.

That night Louis dreamed.

School days floated by, vistas of green playing fields, the far-away sound of children playing: A group, his friends, spinning a medallion: Giggling, jesting, spinning, flashing: The maw opening before him.

Voices, deep, resonant: Louis gazing up at faces, confused faces, anxious.

The smell of grease, machine oil; his first day at work: Taken from the spinning, flashing lathe, to grind down burrs in another part of the factory. His body floated on…

The surgery: He was viewing it from above; could see himself in the chair; the coin dangling before him. The disc spun, came towards him. The vortex…

Words; unintelligible; Stanford scales…susceptible…susceptible…

The very next day he was back. He had woken with a start that morning and arisen early, deciding to get one or two things in town, with the intention of passing through the spaceport to and from work.

On both journeys Louis stopped for a while to amuse the animal with objects he had bought in town or sought out at home. Over the weekend he visited the animal at every opportunity, always bringing a small selection of knick-knacks in which it could find amusement or intrigue. It soon came to recognise Louis' footsteps and would always be trembling with excitement by the time he arrived. When his working week came around again, he allowed himself an extra half-hour in the mornings and often spent more than an hour sitting with the creature at night. His parents, with whom he lived, merely assumed he was putting in some extra work, and rarely questioned his movements.

Had they bothered to look they would have found that Louis was undergoing a subtle change.

The time he spent in the evenings with the animal meant that he had less time to go drinking in the bars, and with the increase in exercise due to the prolonged route through the spaceport each day, Louis was eating more but at the same time, shedding weight. His legs firmed and his abdominal muscles began to show through the decreasing wall of fat around his waist. For the first time in years he ate well; slept better; and found he was coping more with the day's work.

At times Louis tried to analyse his feelings. He had never had any desire to own a pet before and he never allowed himself to forget that one day there would be an empty space where the cage had been; but despite all this he found himself being drawn to the creature in a way that seemed innocuous, yet compelling.

One morning Louis was lucky enough to catch an attendant cleaning out her cage and although the meeting was cold at first, it did give rise to a friendship that Louis strove to nurture.

The attendant too had noticed the strange mesmerism of the creature's eyes and told Louis of a name that had come to him one morning; Meea'. He had no idea where it had come from but it seemed to suit the animal as it was female, and also a rough reproduction of the sound she made.

It was on one such morning, Louis was able to conceal the pen-torch in her bedding and although the attendant would never allow him to touch or stroke Meea', Louis took great delight and pride in the fact that she treasured the gift and would produce it from a secret place in the cage whenever they were alone. It soon became a regular event for Louis to drop off fruit or other tit bits the attendant had discovered she liked, but best of all Louis learned that Meea' would probably be around for a little while yet as the terminal awaited another shipment to join hers.

Over the weeks Louis continued to visit Meea' with increasing regularity. He utilised his lunch breaks, cut short his working day and devoted his entire evening to being with her. No one intervened, or pointed out the dangers.

No one cared.

Over those weeks a passion grew inside Louis that he knew to be insensible yet impossible to expel. She was with him in his dreams, by his side at his work. Together in the evenings with only a slab of glass between them, Louis stared into her eyes, intoxicated now.

It was through his close association with the assistant that Louis finally learnt of Meea's sudden exportation plans.

"Sorry, Louis," he mentioned one morning. "I'm afraid she'll be going soon."

Louis' world stopped. A vacuum encased him.

"Where," he asked, trying to conceal a choke?

"Oh, God knows; can't pronounce the name on the transfer sheet; a new planet somewhere. They've been sending equipment and other bits and pieces for quite a while now. Part of a big colonisation programme, I guess."

"When…" Louis managed?

"A few days yet, Louis: She'll join the rest of the junk in the compound until the shuttles arrive."

"Compound?"

"Over there – Strictly off limits; everything gets a good going over by the security boys before loading."

Louis stared past the attendant to a collection of buildings and high wire fences he had never taken any notice of before. The area looked remote and deserted. Occasionally the crash of metal or the roar of an engine drifted over from the repair yards behind.

"Looks quiet," Louis remarked.

"'Tis usually; although they've been working on this shipment for the last couple of days."

A horn was sounding from one of the yards, announcing the start of the day shift, Louis mused. The engineering yards behind would back onto the compound, he guessed; as he was familiar with the road that ran past the front of them.

He returned to Meea', wondering about the fence separating the two.

At work that afternoon he obtained permission to visit the repair yards; on the pretext of giving an important message to a personal friend. In the huddled engineering community it was common practice for the employee of one firm to wander into another's, to borrow tools or return them, check their instruments or readings against another's, or simply skive. So lax was it that he strode up the hill and round past Protile Industries, turning into the repairs yards without even considering the type of work they did there. No one stopped or questioned him. He felt safe and at ease in his factory overalls, blending in with the environment.

He entered through the gates and followed the main avenue for a hundred meters until some administrative buildings barred his way. Not wanting to stray too near, Louis skirted around them and became somewhat lost in the labyrinth of alleyways beyond.

Louis strode resolutely on, maintaining a bearing of nonchalance and even tedium as he passed by workshops and welding bays; gaining some form of direction from the huge jibs towering over the whole site. He was relieved when the workshops and bays finally surrendered to an untidy area of discarded machinery and heaps of scrap metal. The high piles of scrap were comforting. He could not only lose himself amongst them, but claim a justifiable excuse for being there by appearing to be looking for that odd piece of metal or fitment. Then quite suddenly, the fence appeared. Louis drew back and took cover.

The compound was quiet, unattended. Obviously no one considered the possibility of a break-in profitable. Most of the tools and machinery were everyday items that could be found lying around in any one of the workshops or sites nearby. The specialised equipment or valuables would be under lock and key in the security huts adjoining the station and flight towers beyond.

Shielding his eyes, Louis looked for Meea's cage to the far side of the landing pads and found it almost buried amongst a vast collection of crates and machinery being readied to join her shipment; small forklifts and trucks trundling back and forth. He noted several lights dotted atop the high wire fence, the tracks of a surveillance droid further inside the security compound, and left, snatching up a tiny pump as he went.

"Hello there;" called the attendant the next morning, "about early."

Louis smiled and nodded. "I wondered if you could give her this fruit today. May have to work late tonight so might not see her."

"Sure thing. I'll give it to her now. Just put your boot up against the door will you, make sure she don't get out."

"Come on my darling; look what your friend has brought you!"

Inside the cage the attendant tipped the fruit into a bowl and watched for a while as Meea' sniffed it quizzically and then sat down to enjoy it.

Louis replaced the keys and held the door open.

"There, she'll like that," exclaimed the attendant, straightening.

"Thanks," replied Louis. "I'll try and say goodbye in my dinner time."

Two hours later, sacrificing a coffee break, Louis crossed the factory floor and tripped up two flights of stairs to the locksmiths.

"Busy Frank?"

"Not especially, Louis. What can I do for you?"

"Lost a key, haven't I. I've got a mould though from a spare. I wondered if you could make me another one from it. It's a bit of a tricky one. The inside should be hollow with a diameter and depth of four mill."

"Hm… not the key to your old man's drinks cabinet is it?"

Louis laughed. "No."

"O.K. no sweat. Dinner time be alright?"

"Fine."

"Right – and oh, thanks for that spot of welding the other day. First class!"

"Any time, Frank."

That evening he worked late. At seven when the charge hands and foremen were thin on the ground, he disappeared to revisit the repair yards. This time he had a half-valid reason. Someone needed a pair of sensitised coupling setters and no one could be bothered to go looking for them. Louis had volunteered.

He set off, making a beeline for the yards.

He needed to see them at night.

On the way home that evening, in the cover of the shadows, Louis tried his key. It worked.

The temptation to join her was almost unbearable but Louis reactivated the locks and encouraged her back to the glass.

"Soon," he murmured. "Soon."

The next morning the cage was gone. Louis' heart skipped a beat. He ran up between the huts and out onto the expanse of the storage bays. The place was deserted. From one of the terminals a convoy of forklifts, trucks and loading platforms were trundling out onto the shuttle plain. Louis searched for the attendant but he was nowhere to be seen. The blood rushed to his hands and face. Had the shuttles arrived? What time would they go? What if they came at night?

He had to know!

He left the storage area and walked as calmly as he could to work. Later, in the hubbub of the morning influx he slipped away and back to the spaceport. The dockers would know, they loaded and unloaded the shuttles for God's sake, they'd have to!

He ran the entire length of the perimeter fence and cut back, bursting out onto the plain near the convoy. It would look as if he was late for work and just cutting across.

"Busy, I see," Louis remarked, coming across a driver leaning against the wheel of his vehicle?

"Mm. be busy all day I reckon, got another load to do tomorrow."

"Oh, coming or going?"

"Going, that lot, I think."

"Tch, amazing isn't it, when you think, shipping stuff all that way."

"Waste of time, if you ask me."

"Where's that lot in the compound going?"

"Compound? Oh… God knows, far out somewhere."

"Suppose you'll be working through the night to load that lot?"

"Not me! No, I don't think it's all been checked over yet. Get an early start tomorrow. Shuttles are coming in at nine."

"You work there?"

"Me? No, repair yards behind."

"Ah…"

"Well, better not be late. Bye."

"Take it easy."

'Stars above', Louis thought. *'It will have to be tonight!'*.

The day went by for him in a blur. He ate a good meal and sweet at lunch and washed it down with a massive vitamin and mineral complex. He let a machine in sick bay analyse his blood for viruses and got the nurse to give him the quick once over when she came in that afternoon. In the coffee break he filched a pair of high-quality wire cutters on a visit to the stores, a pocketful of wire clips, and any other items he thought he might need. At four that afternoon he feigned a severe headache and left for home.

Once inside the empty house, Louis vomited.

It had come unexpectedly, feeling as if something had released him. He grasped the basin he had just managed to reach and sagged against it.

Trepidation gnawed at his stomach. Excitement overwhelmed him; Louis was terrified. In that brief moment of clarity the full madness of what he was doing had become apparent.

He turned on the faucet and splashed cold water onto his face.

It was over. His strength returned. Louis felt purged, free from worry, devoid of emotion.

He grabbed a towel and wiped away the water and tears and walked through to the lounge to compose a letter, probably his last.

When his parents came in from work that evening, he was careful not to disrupt the usual routine. He fiddled about in his room for an hour and repaired to the lounge after dinner to stretch out in front of the entertainment centre.

He made sure all was well that night before he left.

The night air was mild and yet at the same time strangely bracing. Louis stood in the driveway and desperately tried to make sense of it all. His confidence had left him again. It was as if he was viewing life through a reel of film and every so often a blank frame would crop up, a single window through which he could see clearly, think rationally. He felt cold and frightened. The immensity of the cosmos above was too wide for anything as miniscule as he. Suddenly his family, friends, places he knew meant everything to him. He sobbed and caught his breath. What was causing him to leave when he had so much? He shivered in the night as his thoughts tried to fathom out something they didn't understand. He vainly tried to separate and equate his feelings and in doing so, found another presence there…

Meea' was waiting.

His verve returned.

Without looking back, Louis left the driveway and walked towards the spaceport.

He cut across the storage area and through the small turnstile, following the road past his factory and continuing onward towards the repair yards. The night shift kept a small gate open and in his overalls he moved through it unquestioned and virtually unnoticed. He was a little overloaded with a rucksack and tool-bag but no one bothered him. Here and there, the flash of a welding set belied the deserted appearance of the yards.

He skirted around the administrative buildings, showing only a light or two, and moved into the scrap area abutting the compound.

A forklift ablaze with lights rolled by up ahead and Louis froze. In the back of his mind he knew the fence would not go unnoticed if there were workmen nearby.

He waited, but it didn't return.

The compound was shrouded in deep shadow, made even darker by the huge sun-pack lights dotted about. Louis crouched behind the same pile of scrap castings and divested himself of his rucksack and equipment. He just had enough shadow by the fence in which to work. The surveillance robot was his only concern.

He looked about and found it trundling around the other side of the compound looking ridiculously slow and ponderous on its stubby caterpillar tracks. He pulled out the wire cutters and, checking each way to see if it was clear, darted up to the fence.

The clippers made a dull 'ping' as the first strand broke and for the first time Louis was grateful of the conglomeration of equipment and machinery spread around in the compound, screening the noise and, he hoped fervently, his actions. By the time he had to take cover he'd done better than expected. Now he would find out if his plan had any credence. Would the surveillance droid spot the cut wire? Louis couldn't from his position amongst the scrap, but he knew with ultra-sensitive scanners the robot could magnify a flea and pinpoint it on the wire if necessary, but it was a machine after all, and the eyes gazing through the monitors human. Something would have to alert it before it scoured the area.

Louis watched it pass by, a part of him wishing almost the forklift would return and confirm his handiwork. Galvanised, he left the security of the slag heap again and made his second and final series of cuts in the wire, praising its rigidity.

The crash of a metal girder as it swung above echoed across the concourses. In the cacophony of shouts from the night shift, Louis shouldered his bags and scampered to the fence to pass everything through.

It was so easy. On the other side there was only a few meters of light left before deep shadow again engulfed him, offering sanctuary. Louis slipped though, scuttling to the safety of the shadows then returned to the fence to straighten it and attach some wire clips to hold it taut.

He had only just ensconced himself in amongst the massive crates of machinery once more when the electric whirr of the surveillance droid pierced the night again.

Concealed in the darkness, Louis watched it pass by, this time from the inside.

He felt cosy and safe amid the collections of crates and machinery. He had passed the first phase. After carefully creeping about, he soon found Meea's cage and began a careful inspection of its exterior. There would be a bright blue splodge from a marker pen if the security men had already checked it over;

this he'd been careful to note from Meea's attendant. But the search became difficult. Although well hidden in amongst the middle of all the cargo, light from an overhead security beacon had caught one corner of the steel box and rather annoyingly crept along the top of it like liquid illumination. With the looming flight control towers close by with several windows ablaze, he was worried he'd be seen. Finally, after checking the position of the security robot, Louis chanced a glance and found what he was looking for, a big bright blue tick smeared across the middle.

Reinforced carbide bolts slid back from their slots. Louis passed in his bags and found Meea' crouched in one corner, waiting for him, her huge eyes glistening. On his knees, they embraced, rubbed noses, and then Louis went to work sealing up the door from the inside.

A rocking sensation woke Louis. Someone yelled.

"Careful with that!"

He realised his legs were lying across the doorway of the sleeping quarters separating Meea's compartments and hastily tucked himself up, trying to conceal them in the straw. Meea' clung to him, wild-eyed with fright.

"Put that cage over with the others lads; don't want Chimy all shook up in the take off!"

Louis felt the cage lurch and come to rest with a bump. It entered shadow as it was wheeled along a ramp and then into a cargo bay of one of the shuttles.

"Think we ought to check on her," a voice asked, alarmingly close to the cage?

"Naw, she'll be alright. Come on; let's get the rest of the stuff aboard."

All day the loading went on; it was late in the afternoon when an ominous silence fell over the compound. The shuttle's bay doors closed with a bang, and the hold was plunged into darkness. Much later, lights winked on one by one and someone came to check on Meea' – and all the other animals travelling with her. Louis had panicked but found the hatch door jammed up against another crate. He hid in the sleeping compartment until the lights went out again.

A deafening roar exploded beneath them. A whine sifted through the craft as one by one, like ugly great insects, the shuttles lifted from the ground.

Captain Malloway was watching from a window as the shuttles floated up to meet him. Two years with InterWorld Cargos – and most of the time had been spent in stasis, going back and forward from the same place. He was sick of the job already. Voni Singleton, the crew's bio-medic made him jump.

"Hi, Cap; nice vacation?"

Malloway grunted; "Alright, I suppose. What conglomeration of rubbish have we got this time?"

"The usual; seismographic equipment; drilling platforms; some generators of various kinds; literally tons of seeds and plantlets."

He snorted. "When are they going to start shipping people out there, that's what I want to know? I'd stay awake for a trip then instead of those goddamn tubes."

"I know what you're thinking," the bio-medic leered. "They'll all be scientists and high-brows, definitely not your type. Anyway I doubt the authorities will like it if the colonisation gets underway with lots of little Malloways."

The captain grunted again. "Probably right."

"What are you going to do; we've got some livestock on this trip, haven't we?"

"Mmm, thought I might sit my C.F.s again. Failed them last year."

"Tch."

"Why don't you do the same. Be glad of the company."

"Na, biology isn't my thing. Anyway Jeff and Paul will be with you. I'd only be in the way. Well, let's go check it all in shall we?"

In the solitude of their cage, Louis and Meea' listened as the forklifts trundled towards them. One by one the cages, crates and pallets of equipment and machinery were removed from the shuttles and placed accordingly in the cavernous hold of the ship. Unlike the hold of the shuttle, the ship's bays were brightly lit and Louis was unsure if he had escaped detection as he slipped from the cage not long after being set down, hiding behind some taller ones.

From a safe distance Louis watched as a figure clad in a green and white suit and another in uniform stood beside Meea's cage.

"Only one," asked Malloway, glancing at the crystal information panel?

"Yes, for now apparently. The first specimen of a completely new order of ape. Extremely rare. Only discovered recently on some backwater planet.

Classification is still in progress. Would you believe it was the only primate the team discovered there?"

"Go on."

"True, they scoured vast areas of the planet – not another primate in their order. No other monkeys, apes, orangutans or lemurs. Nothing, not even shrews. They were eating themselves out of existence, on the verge of extinction."

"Oh."

"Mm, some genetic disorder or something, just weren't mating anymore. It was hoped this one female might be introduced into a troop of chimps or sloths on this new planet."

Malloway caught a glimpse of the animal at her doorway of its straw-filled retreat. He didn't know why, but those wide alien eyes sent a shiver through his body.

***

"Here's to a good trip," the second navigations officer called out, raising his glass! Half the crew took a gulp from various vessels. Voni Singleton raised hers and winked at Malloway.

"Sleep tight," she called as he rose to follow the other crew members to the stasis tubes.

"See you at the other end," he called over his shoulder.

Meanwhile the four hundred thousand tonne ship glided effortlessly out of the solar system and filliped away into the void.

In the hold, unaware of the planet they were leaving, Louis and Meea' embarked on a voyage all of their own.

A year passed swiftly. In it, the ship straddled the vast distances. Voni Singleton gained her certificates and, biologically speaking, Captain Malloway only slept for two months of his life.

Throughout the voyage Louis had managed to escape detection. It hadn't been easy but Voni

Singleton's tenacity for routine had helped. The cage had become their home, the other animals their neighbours – they were no longer frightened of Louis. They accepted him. By robbing them of a little of their supplies each day, he had managed to sustain himself. His ration packs too had helped but he had also been using his own supply of bodily reserves and they were now all but depleted. The specialised diet of Meea's to which he had become accustomed, could not sustain them for much longer. It was more by coincidence than guesswork that, on the last few days of the voyage, Louis decided to show himself.

It was early morning, ship's time. Voni Singleton walked down the corridors and into the hold to tend her wards. Meea' being the biggest arthropod was normally the first to receive her attention.

"Hi, Meea' – the name had come to her also. "Guess what I've got for you this morning. Avello fruit. Nice, eh?"

Louis advanced, leaving a section of the cargo area that had been his refuge for so long.

"Ers, misss…"

The bio-medic whirled, dropping the container of fruit.

She thought she was going to faint at first, but her professional bearing kept her erect. "My word…What – who are you?"

He found it difficult to pronounce his name. "Loo – Loo –is, miz. A stoo-wo… a stow-a-way."

"Alright, alright –" hands out to pacify. "– just stay there. I'll get help."

Voni Singleton ran the half mile to the living quarters.

"Stowaway!" Captain Malloway stared into the bio-medic's face as if she'd just turned to stone. He was looking for the slightest trace of amusement but Voni Singleton's face was continuing to register the shock and fright it had first shown when she burst into the recreation lounge.

"What's up," asked one of the crew members now clustering round?

"Break out some light side arms," barked Malloway, "and follow me."

The crew stood in the cargo hold, some embarrassed by the weapons they were totting, and stared at Louis. This was crazy. They didn't have anything in the operations manual about this – hell, InterWorld Cargos weren't going to like it either!

Malloway holstered his pistol. "What's your name son?"

"Looo-iss, Lou-is, serr…"

"He's having problems with articulation, probably lack of food."

"Lack of food!" – Hell, look at him. Diz, get in touch with Alpha, tell 'em what's going on. Can he do any damage in here, Lem?"

"No, best leave him where he is. He obviously wants to be with chimpy."

"Alright. Voni, seal this section until we get the score on this."

***

"Ok. Let me have it." Malloway slumped into a couch and cracked a can of beer. The crew had assembled a half hour before to hear the news.

"It's not good, cap. We've been put in stasis. A specialist team is on its way out here from Deimos."

"How long?"

"Could be six weeks."

The crew groaned.

"What about our friend?"

"Just says 'leave him. Don't interfere.' They're quarantined of course."

"Anything else?"

"No, says 'just sit tight'."

"Wonderful."

"Fancy another set of lectures, Lem?"

"Might as well."

Malloway went back to sleep.

It took nearly two months for the team to arrive. By then it was too late.

Legal Courts; Earth.

"And I conclude m'lord, that although Louis Barns was under some influence when he wrote this letter, it remains that he was acting – as far as we can judge – on his own intentions when he primarily solicited the attentions of the aforementioned creature. It only leaves me to record a verdict of misadventure."

On the other side of the galaxy, Meea's planet was pin-pointed and duly quarantined. The team were lifted off.

Back in orbit around planet A113B4 the colonisation went ahead as planned but by no human hand. It would be given a wide berth from now on.

On the planet surface Malloway stood by the windows of a shuttle and stared out at a strange new world.

"What in God's name happened, Voni?"

"A kind of hypnosis, I felt it myself. The person only had to be willing or a little susceptible, and the creature did the rest. Amazing."

"What about him?"

"Complete metamorphis; skeletal; skin; hair, blood cells, the lot. A sort of regression to the animalistic state. Incredible."

"Did they have to turn the whole goddamn planet over to them?"

The bio-medic shrugged. "He's still expressing an intelligence of sorts. Could be dangerous to dump them back with her kind. I don't think anybody wants to take the responsibility just yet. Anyway, it'll be interesting, a new strain. Just think Cap; in years to come you'll be able to say you had a hand in it."

"Yea, but suppose they don't…you know?"

The bio-medic smiled. "We ran some tests. That's one happy couple out there."

In the evanescing steam of the shuttles, Meea' took her first tentative steps onto a strange new world. Moments later, Louis emerged; raised his feline face to the sky and followed her down the ramp.

Furred hand clutched furred hand as ape huddled ape on the alien soil.

"Hey, look at that!" exclaimed a crew member as they moved into the jungle.

He'd just caught the gleam of an old pen-torch held tightly in Meea's hand.

The End

The Internet girls

Faith and Trust

From:**Katy.Brianty**(KatyBrianty67.Aus.Earth.
@InterSpacial.Web.com)

Sent: 26 November 2289. 0400:09:32

To: Todd40009@InterSpacialWeb.com

"I love you baby; love like a rose needs summer and rain. My love is everlasting, transcending space and time – oh baby my love is for you and u alone you are my love and hardship. Be your woman and soul mate and kiss and hug all time and you have big love all ways. My love is built on trust and you need to trust to love, but you need to love first, to smile with your heart and to know one another. One important thing is to let each other go if you can't do this. Love is a wonderful thing of compassion and satisfaction and should be given respect and trust. We work at it, yes? I know becos i will care for you and you will share my skin wen we wake and in morning and all through the day, go with the ups and downs with you – is that all right, baby?"

'You can go up and down on my dick any time you like darling;' drools Todd, for the third time that day, ogling the pictures of the scantily clad buxom female spread across the top of his screen.

A scuttling and scratching at the doorway interrupts him and Navigations Officer Todd represses the urge to continue to listen intently. Since the final demise of the ship's crew months ago – save him and Gem, the colony of rats and mice surviving somehow in the bowels of the ship have grown exponentially and have got bolder and bolder, and soon they'll overrun the place if something's not done.

'They'll eat anything,' he remembers, one zoological expert telling him, months – years ago, as he closes one message down to attend to another. *'Cardboard; Wood; Wiring; even chewing through*

thin metal to get at something inside; Voracious little buggers!'

They would soon raid the ship's larders and store containers if they hadn't already, he muses; a surplus of food with no-one now to eat it. The animals in the bio-spheres having to be culled twice annually, the carcasses mercifully ejected.

From:LovethOssy.Lovebean51.Nigera.SouthAfrica@InterSpacialWeb.com

Sent: 26 Nov 2289 0400: 23: 14

To: Todd40009@InterSpacialWeb.com

'Did not hear from you last night my darling love. Is everything alright? Of course my love is for you and you alone, I'd never dream of hurting you the way I've been let down; but don't worry I'm here for you no matter the huge distances. it's really as if I'm right there beside you, holding you, letting my body warm you in the cold reaches of space. Love is like a light fresh summer rainfall my love and is such a wonderful gift. You have to trust me on this as I trust you and of course trust binds the very fabric of love together to form a beautiful union. Remember my love, being honest with each other is everything. Someone can be as special on the outside as they are on the inside but when he or she betrays your trust they become the ugliest person in the world. Love is patient. Love is kind. It does not envy. It does not boast. It is not proud. It is not rude. It is not self-seeking. It is not easily angered. It keeps no record of wrong doing. It does not delight in evil, but perseveres. True love takes many things. It always protects, trusts, hopes, wishes, dreams, and points to everything you've got, even when you think it's not going to be enough. Love, my darling Tod is not always fireworks and shooting stars; sometimes it is simple understanding and trust between two people.'

'Bye for now Tod; you're forver in my dreams. XXXX'

'Write soon. X Loveth.'

Todd stretches in his seat having been kept rapt for several minutes, wondering at the poignant sentiments. *'It's poetic,'* he thinks, impressed by how eloquent and warm the women back on Earth are – *and write; and feel!* He wants to emulate them, scribe candid but meaningful letters, messages full of sincerity and harmony; but his diction is awful; terse and without honesty and any real sense of love or empathy, and now he has no one to teach him, the ship's computers cold and as analytical as any class three droid.

Yet the women respond with such vigour and outpourings of the soul, ignoring his pathetic attempts at a decent reply; page upon page of the most heart-rending passion it's not hard to imagine they are far-flung relatives, perhaps in some small way to such literary greats as Jane Austen or the Brontë sisters.

His mind drifts; he imagines being back on Earth – transported back in time somehow to the eighteenth century where people are still speaking the old dialect in perfect punctuation and observing every propriety.

Todd scrolls back in time to a particular woman who penned some beautiful scripts as if from Wordsworth himself, then quite suddenly disappearing from the airways without explanation or goodbye; and after what had become a wonderfully romantic liaison, lasting nearly a full month; the punch line for money (as with many obvious on-line scams) not coming until he himself offered to help. Her father was very ill in hospital apparently in former Vietnam although it did not at first come out in conversation; only much later when he pointedly asked about her direct family.

He was so heartbroken for her he racked his brains as to how to release his funds and somehow transfer them, but after traipsing about the ship and viewing the wrecked and damaged sections of the vessel for himself it was evident all secondary systems had been closed down in order to preserve the primary.

He had wandered about in a mental daze for hours afterwards – even asking Gem for help but her accounts were frozen too and anyway she had no real belief in his paramours no matter how genuine.

Perhaps her father had truly died; he mused idly; sitting slumped at his console. Perhaps she'd taken off with what little estate her father had left, starting afresh someplace else. Pity, he thought, recalling a line from one of Lianna's communiqués; *'Dear, you are the bright blue ocean in which I swim; gliding and floating as if born again; my skin rippling with agitation as your waves caress and surround me; I wallow in you tenderness and warm embrace and swim and pirouette and jump and gambol with joy in your shallows, laughing and chattering just as the dolphins do.'*

'I am yours, my sweet.'

'If you can send money my dear, here is my address…'

Todd draws in a heartfelt sigh and shifts his weight in his seat again.

He wrote back explaining his situation, wanting desperately to express his loneliness and utter despair at being left alone with only one other companion, someone who hated him as much as she annoyed and irritated Todd. He tried to talk about the stark emptiness of the ship and the frightening gulf of the crushing vacuum called space outside that was enough to drive you mad if you let it. He hoped to convey how the haunting echoes of the souls that once inhabited the colossal vessel – all nine hundred and sixty three of them – still murmur sibilant whispers to anybody that wants to hear. He taps into them sometimes on the ship's vacant intercoms, strange static-filled, garbled utterances and sometimes what sounds like commands or urgent memos, all mixed up and calling as if they are actually in the hulk's ether rather than emanating from the speakers. He wants to tell his friends and confidants all this, but can't find the right words no matter how he tries: was just not versed or trained in romantic logorrhoea or verbose rhetoric.

He does his best however, desperate to eke out a seminal piece of poetry in an effort to converse with someone his innermost feelings; couching words and sentences and deleting them again in a never-ending edit. Gem and Todd tried everything at first, once the last of the deceased crew had been put into a vacuumed storage area; tennis; playing the piano; guitar lessons; chess; some sports, but in the end he found his true avocation at a computer terminal – internet dating.

Not what you might call an academic pastime, but what the hell, there was no-one left to tell him otherwise, no-one, or thing above him in rank, not even directives from Earth now or even the orbiting space stations.

'Why don't you turn that bleeding thing off?'

Gem has somehow crept up behind him, with stealth and cunning, a very faint aroma of the most sensual perfume lingering in the air. He breathes deep of the lovely smell and is mellowed for a moment.

"Space, honey; Space and time."

"Oh, Jeeze..!"

Gem stalks nearer.

'I'm here for you, you know, you bad-smelling hunk of jelly.'

His console bleeps and his messaging centre alerts him to the fact that a response he was waiting for from the voluptuous Katy Brianty has arrived.

"Hush honey – I think I've actually got a pull!"

Gem snorts – full of venom. 'A fucking pull. You sad sod – all you are going to pull in this shithole is the wrong lever and decompress the whole stinking wreck – not that that wouldn't be a bad thing!'

She bristles and radiates with hatred beside him, arms akimbo. Todd purses his lips and twists his mouth and wonders whether to activate the screen or not, his fingers hovering over the elaborate keyboard.

He glances around, almost expectantly, as if parts of the immense ship will tear apart at any moment and the whole ecosystem disintegrate. The port nacelle and superstructure has already decided to detach itself, cracks in the accelerating array becoming suddenly worse; the main engine faltering just after that so the ship slewed sideways and shot off crookedly on a course all of its own. Some kind of mysterious flu virus did for the entire crew some weeks later, as if the jinxed crate was doomed from the very start. Isolated groups held out for a while but the virus seemed highly virulent and air-born; all dying in a matter of months.

Without proper navigation – the systems failures affecting nearly all the vessel in some way or other – they were soon lost. Now, drifting ever further from the last beacons, never mind the small colonial solar system, there seems little hope of rescue or retrieval, the owners cutting their losses and consigning the survey ship to its fate.

'You have no soul – no interest,' he quips, bringing himself back to the present; his fingers still hovering!

'WHAT," Gem straightens beside him, indignation lining her face, shaking her pretty head? "Listen pea brain. I've cared for you all these goddamn months – years, clearing up after you and your goddamn mess, being your sex toy when you get lonely, playing all your stupid games; dressing for you, calling you; *'My Partner', 'soul mate'* – you bastard! And now you have the temerity to canvas emails from some dead star – Madge! Don't that take it?"

"It's far from dead, honey; and anyway, it's only a bit of harmless fun, darling."

"Don't 'darling' me, you loser!"

Todd sighs theatrically.

"Turn it off!"

Frustration builds; Todd bangs the console with one fist and shakes his head. He senses Gem moving for him and although the computer screens are protected he quickly hides them; screen and keypad disappearing rapidly under inch thick shields.

He braces himself for a set to, but before the argument can turn nasty Andrilick, a second stage droid Professor Hylm Robertman was working on in his last days, enters and hovers hesitantly.

Gem turns to address him and Todd twists in his chair. Andrilick was the professor's last creation, and the eminent professor must have been in two minds, or half senile, the robot having both male and female attributes, as androgynous as a fairy queen in a South Australian pantomime. It doesn't matter too much about the masculine torso, broad shoulders, or the somewhat ungainly arms and hands, or that the automaton has shapely hips and legs which taper down to exquisite ankles; it's the head, with its integration of pseudo-organic coverings and nexus of sheathed inputs: the cellular structure of a fully functioning face is the problem. Pre-programming in the glandular subroutines went somewhat awry in the last stages of its development, and right now the poor thing looks like a cross between a Mongol raider and a Swedish masseur; the white blonde hair that sweeps down from one side of the head, almost covering one eye, is tied back with a clip, and has been chopped mercilessly while his attempt to shave the clumps of course black bristle over the majority of its face has failed miserably. The lenses of the sparkling emerald eyes flick about nervously.

He's not that tall, but even so Todd issued him a severe reprimand to create a warning jingle after he nearly gave him a small heart attack, looming out of the darkness once when the lighting in a particular corridor suddenly failed.

"What is it, Andri'" Gem asks, the tension between him and her evaporating a little, thankfully?

Andrilick holds hands with himself diffidently and proclaims, "Lunch is to be served."

'Lunch,' thinks Todd. He glances at a clock and realises he's been at the console for the last three hours.

Blazing suns! Where'd the morning go?

"Come on then," he grumbles; "let's get this fiasco over with."

"What! So you can get back to your girlfriends?"

Todd pauses, but doesn't rise to the bait.

The two follow the second stage droid like a small funeral procession and enter the nearby dinner suite.

The room is opulent, kept meticulously clean and sparkling by the serving droids who have nothing better to do now. The plastic chandeliers sparkle and gleam above and the fake wood paneling and cupboards housing the stainless steel cutlery glisten with layer upon layer of real beeswax. The rich carpeting has been specially vacuumed and freshened and chemical candles burn here and there giving the room a very romantic feel.

Gem and Todd take their seats, a small child-sized robot helping Todd with his chair.

The large oval table is of real wood with an expensive veneer, laid out for the captain and senior staff once, although Todd and Gem only sit at one end now, opposite one another.

After they've got comfortable, Gem picks the fan-folded serviette from the holder and begins to straighten it out, then re-fold it. It's something she does each and every breakfast, lunch, and dinner time, a kind of obsessive or cathartic manipulation of cloth that seems to occupy her mind for a while or otherwise entertain her, sometimes making quite interesting designs and others just playing with it. This evening Todd watches on with interest, as, after folding and re-folding it, she crumples it up in her dainty hands and leaves it sitting on the placemat totally disheveled.

Todd frowns, sitting straight, his hands in his lap.

"Guessed what it is yet," Gem asked without looking up at him?

Todd narrows his eyes and sighs inwardly. After a moment he shakes his head. "A mess?"

"Close," Gem avers. "Chaos." And she smiles with smug confidence.

Todd considers. After twisting his mouth, he reaches for his serviette.

He unfolds it, then laying it flat, rolls it over into a long sausage. He twists and bends it until it resembles an 'S' shape, turning it sideways.

It's Gem's turn to frown now.

"Old dollar sign – without the two central strokes," she enquires?

Todd purses his lips and shakes his head. "Wrong way up."

Gem cocks her head and screws her face up into a question mark. It's comical to Todd as he studies her, as if for the first time, and for a moment he is lost in her beauty; enamoured. Her blonde hair is saffron yellow, iridescent in the glowing candle light. Eyes are of the brightest blue, the little retroussé nose small and almost cute. Her lips are full and plump, while glowing white teeth complete her gorgeous looks. Always there is colour in her cheeks. Her shoulders are slim and feminine, hands delicate and pristine.

Todd's gaze drifts down, taking in her small breasts, the thin sports bra and chiffon top she wears, allowing the aurora and nipples to show through.

It's enticing; Todd admiring her through slanted eyes.

Gem has put a fist under her chin, plonking an elbow on the table, considering the conundrum. Eventually she gives up.

"Sine wave," Todd explains, and unravels the cloth to lay it by his hand.

"That's silly."

"No more daft than your 'chaos'.

The first course arrives, baulking any more argument.

Andrilick, serviette over one arm, places a small bowl in front of Gem and removes the thin lid. Steam rises, evanesces into the atmosphere.

Gem savours the aroma by waving her nose over the steaming bowl.

"Smells delicious Andri. What is it?"

"Cream soup of wild mushroom, Mam, with ravioli of truffles on foie gras."

The small boy-droid has placed a similar bowl at Todd's sitting but he waves it away with annoyance.

Gem has already taken a spoon, and preparing herself vigorously by wriggling excitedly in her seat, bends to taste it gently, scooping it correctly from the side of her bowl, blowing a little.

"Mmm," she murmurs moments later, then looks up to find Todd's is being taken away.

Gem implodes, sighing audibly, shaking her head. "You could at least try it! I expect the class two and threes have been out in the domes all day, searching for the mushrooms and truffles."

Todd snorts. "Too much liquid gives me gas anyway, you know that," He folds his arms, trying to find something in the room with which to occupy his mind.

What was once verdant woodlands and lush rainforests out in the massive domes mid-ships must have since dwindled and shrivelled to a collection of desiccated tombs by now, he reminisces, the last rays of Rigel fading fast as the ship, now on a course all of its own, sailed inexorably past.

Gem finishes her soup and pats her lips with the serviette, scowling across at Todd. His ire is up and he unfolds his arms to place an elbow and clenched fist on the table, allowing his ring finger to extend and wriggle a little.

She glances at him, raising her eyebrows in mock surprise, lowering her vision to ignore him, rearranging her cutlery with a nonchalant air.

"I'm heartened to see you can keep something up," she mutters under her breath.

Fuck You!

Todd glares at her, crestfallen; beaten yet again. He shakes his head and drops his hand.

It's always the same, he muses. She has to have the last word, no matter if she's right or wrong.

He raps his fingertips on the placemat dismissing it, and wonders for the umpteenth time why, when he can receive mail from lonely women back on Earth, why have Starfleet neglected them? The beacons they've deployed along the way are all still working – as far as he knows, and the ship still has dozens to use, so why? Are they just too far out now for a rescue mission or salvage? Or has the ship been quarantined and left to its' own devices? The strange virus was indeed virulent, deadly; killing without mercy; almost one hundred percent success rate, although even pathogens, he knew, had the sense to leave one or two of their prey alive otherwise they'd have nothing to feed on in the future. Basic law of survival, he cogitates, mete out your rations.

The second course arrives. Tinned ballotines of chicken, stuffed with crab (from storage) and ginger, on a tomato and garlic sauce.

Todd marvels at the imagination eyeing the preparation skeptically. The lump of chicken looked expertly cooked, the skin a golden brown and the sauce smells delicious. He nods appreciatively and takes hold of his utensils, the second class droids retreating to hover close by. He cuts into the meat, which falls apart almost and scooping a little sauce brings it to his mouth, bending forward a little.

The meat is tasteless however, only the garlic sauce saving the day, a slight savoury meaty tang energising his mouth. The stuff out of storage is always the same, he contemplates, chewing effortlessly; watered down effigies of what they once were.

He wonders whether there are any chickens left, since they haven't had an egg in a while?

His communication bracelet beeps and Todd checks his emails, finding all are from his paramours back on Earth, poor lonely souls who, even in the twenty third century are still on the bread line apparently and living from week to week. He can't send them any money since his accounts were frozen months ago when the ship started to fall apart, the treasury and banking outlets all on a floor that got flooded with radiation.

He pulls his cuff back over his bracelet with indifference and allows the small droid behind to collect his plate.

"All *lovey dovey,* are we," Gem sneers?

"Shut up…"

"None from Starfleet, I take it?"

Todd shakes his head. He takes a sip of wine, a fine Chianti from a region of France back on Earth but it's as insipid as his chicken and he wonders for the umpteenth time why they bother with these daft charades.

Gem smacks her lips and peruses the small menus that have been prepared and left beside their serving mats.

"Whole poached pear with a leek and Roquefort Mousse and watercress cream," she reads with ardent rapture.

Todd stifles a sigh and rolls his eyes; wanting to get back to the console. It's their only connection with Earth, for crying out loud, so he feels compelled to keep in touch. Etiquette demands he remain in his seat however, until Gem is ready to depart. She knows this and will sometimes hang it out deliberately just for spite. It infuriates him although he tries to hide it most times.

Lunch over with; Todd retreats with haste to his office while Gem, inspecting the ends of her honeyed hair and beige nails still at the table, decides both could do with a little attention.

***

Todd reseats himself at his console and activates it, punching in his code. There's another message from the delectable Katy and he can't wait to read it.

'Oh baby, if ur skin was close to mine – you'd know what love *and* sex is because you're my man and I will care and fondle u till the stars above wink out and blackness engulfs us. We'll roll through the vacuum and make love like whales and caress and play and roll in the surf of the universe and make love over and over again. Baby never let me go. Make me urs. Oh lo…

'If you can send me some money baby no matter how much, because I'm not here to play games or deceive you, just want you to be happy but I need a little money darling for food as you know my dear budgie died two days ago and the funeral cost 200 dollars so if you can get it to me soon I will be forever grateful. Please don't let me down baby, please.'

'Yours FORVER KATY.'

Todd reads it again and cogitates. He has no idea how big a budgerigar is but it must have been substantial to rack up two hundred dollars in funeral costs. He makes a mental note to ask Gem, thinking it will be a good talking point over dinner later, but then decides against it. Anything to do with his illicit pastime is definitely not for the dining table.

He thinks up a reply of sorts, trying to explain his dilemma; the ship crippled; the crew dead; his funds frozen, and then attends to other messages.

He's wading his way through a particularly long one from a Chinese girl in the Panyam province when a paragraph arrests his attention. *'You are like the big blue ocean in which I swim, gliding and floating free as if born again. My skin ripples with agitation as your waters caress and surround me. I wallow in your tenderness and warm embrace and dive and pirouette and jump and gambol in your shallows, laughing and chattering just as the dolphins do.'*

Hang on, Todd thinks. He's read that someplace else. Suspicious, he reopens Lianna's post box and scrolls back through her messages. Sure enough, after reading a certain script he had highlighted, the words are almost identical.

How's that possible, he thinks, naively, dispiritedly: Unless the girls are somehow networking and borrowing scripts from one another. Both women live in or near the Xian, Shaanxi province, so it's likely he contemplates, still a little dejected.

He is so lost in the whys and wherefores he is unable to respond to the urgent intercom signal until he realises it's from Gem.

"We've got a problem," she tells him.

"We've got several," he responds thinking she's alluding to their psychoanalytical comparisons.

"I'm not talking about us, you moron. Just get down here will you?"

"Down where? I'm not a mind-reader."

"The crypts and cold storage sections. It should throw a bit of light on why you are apparently receiving messages from Earth when Starfleet has decided to neglect us."

Puzzled, Todd closes down his terminal and leaves his seat to cycle the vast corridors of the ship.

Down in the crypts and converted cold storage areas, Gem, with a small retinue of various service and maintenance droids are scrutinising an opened hatch near a massive computer terminal. Inside, as

Todd parks his bike and strolls over, three droids are knee-deep in wiring and cabling.

"What's going on," he asks?

Gem walks over to the cold storage area, originally designed to house all the slaughtered animals for future consumption, but now acting as a hanger sized tomb, the bodies, as directed by the pathological directives, laid out on the floor and shelving like so many bundles of meat, none touching the other, frigid air allowed to circulate and freeze any germs.

Gem kicks at a chewed hole right in the corner of a section of wall near the stainless door. Down by her small boot, droppings of some sort are strung out near the ragged opening.

"The rats or mice have chomped their way through the thin metal and through inches of insulation and yet another layer of thin metal on the other side to feast on the bodies no doubt."

Todd nods with a vacant stare. Droids trundling a welding machine up the corridor arrest his attention and he watches with idle interest as another is making a rough approximation with a tape measure.

He sniffs with irritation. "Was it really necessary," he wonders, "to drag me all the way down here?"

Gem smirks with a decisive glint in her eye. Todd doesn't like the look.

"There's more," she continues with devious glee; and ushers him over to the computer room hatch.

"Seems a droid, or more likely a technician, didn't shut the hatch properly last time they were down here, and guess what..?"

Todd, whose been eyeing the hatch with staid scrutiny, twists his head to stare at Gem.

"What?"

"The mice – and whatever else – have been chewing their way through bundles of cables and wiring and the short circuiting has been corrupting the neural retention discs of the crew."

"Retention discs?"

"The entire crew's memories had to be kept on file for future reference; the short circuits have energised several and through the various interfaces with the ship's own computers has been siphoning off nearly all one section of females and relaying the information to other inboard subroutines, just as one would talk to another. You've been responding to the ship's disabled interfaces and the ship has been responding to you, obviously thinking it's carrying out a fundamental task."

Gem cannot, no matter how much she tries, keep the next sentence free from sarcastic humour.

"Do you want to chat away now (smirk), while you're here (giggle), any last requests – things like that, (hand quickly to mouth), before I shut this section down. (Chuckle, chuckle.)"

Todd's eyes glaze over. His mind goes into the vacancy of a mental breakdown.

He wants to punch something.

Gem seems like a most excellent idea but he represses the instinct and straightens, arching his back as he's seen so many humans do. He can't think of anything to say, so just about turns and heads back to his bike to cycle forlornly all the way to the captain's office which he commandeered once everybody had gone; his one break from tedium, his one salvation from going stark raving mad aboard this rotting junkyard now stripped from him.

Gem finds him later sitting at the terminal, but it's not on. She struts over cautiously and stands over him.

"You've still got me," she offers at length.

It's enough to make him fake tears. It's all too much; the thought that he was actually engaging with humans – on a human level, was as exciting as anything he had done before – eliciting, he thought naively, a response from at least some of them.

He stands abruptly, pushing back the chair, realising dimly what a young boy must feel like when he's had his puppy taken from him or his best toy, and finds frustration building in his otherwise detuned cortex. He can't bring forth the words to convey his sorrow, doesn't really understand it, but it's there all the same, the parameters of his encoded mind starting to break away, eating at his artificial soul.

Gem can't rationalise; cannot feel his pain. She tries to console him in the only way she knows and endeavours to cradle him. Todd tries to push her off.

They stumble…

And soon rage boils to the surface.

He's never felt the emotion before, never had to put it to use. He knows he's wrong, even as he raises his fist to swing a punch and even as it is launched and it connects, to propel Gem backwards into the room, making her crash into a far wall as she back-peddles, he knows he's over-stepped the mark.

He staggers over, overrides calming him down. Tears creep into his eyes.

All that passion, all those lovely poetic words and phrases, they are all here, he thinks, right before me: Wrapped up in this one female construct; compassion, tenderness, love and devotion.

Gem has it all, because after all her class one droid nameplate spelling out General Entertainment Model is plain to see, now her blouse has been ripped open. His shirt too is askew. He looks down at her after standing there totally dumbstruck.

Gem simpers in the only way she knows how: Little teardrops well in the bottom of her lovely eyes.

He is mortified. He holds out a hand and she holds out hers, wiping the water away, a small tear in her synthetic skin marring her beautiful features.

It can be fixed, he sighs internally as he lifts her gently to her feet, her fingers caressing his own name plate, reminding him off his ancestry. Terrestrial Off-world Defensive Droid.

"We'll make it," he tells her, holding her close, cradling her. "I've learnt so much from our mentors, I know I can learn much more."

"Trying to love and respect me is all you can do soldier boy. It's all I want."

Todd looks down at her and winks, remembering something from one of the internet girls.

"'Forgiveness is the essence of love,'" he quotes, "even in our artificial world."

"We are, after all, Class Ones!"

The End

The Gardener

"Water, water, anybody," cried Rulelis, joyfully?

'Yes, we do', trilled the hybrid begonias deep in his mind!

Rulelis smiled to himself, wandering over, climbing the plastic steps to the many-tiered gantries, grasping his heavy watering can. He leaned to reach the containers, sprinkling the richly graminaceous liquid over the baby plants, gently and with loving care, swaying the rose back and forth; then relaxed, straightening, gazing out over the rows.

The ship's drones had been helping him all that morning, and all the leaves were sparkling with dewdrops, the seeding compost nice and damp, just right, not waterlogged.

'Thankyou', the begonias cheeped telepathically.

He smiled again, wafting valuable carbon dioxide over his babies, knowing that in this nursery biosphere the youngsters were always thirsty for everything; food; light; moisture.

For too long the ship had been in transit, he mused, stepping away and down, although the voyage had taken them near new stars – they had been at a distance, the light meagre, The Gardener insisting the ship pause in its peregrination to circle a lone yellow orb for a while to allow struggling specimens to revitalise their growth.

The epiphytes of the broadleaved jungle domes had suffered the worst, he'd noticed on his rounds, the huge towering redwoods, eucalyptus, and oaks shadowing the lower regions. But now with the ship in a stable orbit, the craft rotating softly, the gardens and forests would all receive a healthy amount of radiation; the alien glancing up at a nearby graph to see the nanometres were creeping up – 699 and counting; almost at optimum saturation – the point at which absorption and chemical reaction could take place within the green and ochre leaves, producing the much needed sugars and starches.

He climbed back down, taking his time and flowed over to a watering station to refill his can.

Rulelis watched as the spangles of ice cold liquid splashed into his plastic holder, water that had been gleaned from huge chunks of ice asteroids as they'd passed through a planetary belt, filtered and then pumped around the ship. He nearly always found the space ice had a metallic taste, but the other plants loved its purity, so the siphoned water from the lakes of their last planetary survey was all his.

He glanced up and around, aware of something as a shadow shot by behind him.

He reached over and turned off the water, and stepped away, turning to glance about – the movement causing concern. The droids and drones wandered methodically, and apart from the odd fauna he was totally alone on the ship, or up till now he had been.

Rulelis imagined he'd sensed a presence days before in another dome, but couldn't be sure. The ship had surveyed some small island land masses of two oceanic worlds only recently, dropping spores and seeds that might find purchase on the rocky outcrops, and just after breaking orbit, he experienced movement following him around the ship, as if a ghost of a previous worker had somehow materialised to inspect his work.

Rulelis consulted several droids but they reported nothing untoward, and at length and having inspected the biosphere from every perspective, climbing several high points, he dismissed it, telling himself he might have been mistaken.

He continued on his rounds, travelling to the next dome and flouncing through the air lock, then was brought up sharp by the crumpled and dead stump of a once ornamental Acer!

Rulelis was heartbroken.

The twenty foot tall tree had stood in pride of place before the pond for years in a complete space of its own, proud and stately, showing off its reflection in the still, calm waters of the woodland water setting.

Devastated he glided forward.

It had not been overshadowed, nor deficient in any way, he cogitated, moving closer, calculating the substructure of the soil it had sat in, knowing it was correctly managed, having the right ph acidity and just the right amount of humus, the little ferns and small larches and spruces providing the perfect backdrop.

So what amid the stars had killed it, he worried.

He listed carefully over to where several droids were examining the stump, Rulelis immediately suspicious, a fully grown tree, unable to break down and crumble in less than twenty hours – two of his working shifts, yet as he shuffled around it, it was evident every molecule of water had been sucked from the remains, right down to the inner xylem, reducing the once magnificent tree to a crumbling stump. The phloem cells had undergone serious dehydration, he realised staring on, while the protective periderm and thin cork cambium were only one stage from returning to their original carbon. There was almost nothing left of the crowning branches and certainly nothing remaining of the beautiful red leaves save a ghostly filament here and there lying about the ground; as if every ounce of goodness had been extracted from the organism.

Strange, he had to conclude sadly, still crestfallen over its death.

"Droids," he almost barked, "take soil samples, check air density – and for pollutants – and precipitation, I want a full analysis!"

He glanced around, then bent to inspect the surrounding ground suspiciously, bending and digging into the humus carefully and uprooting tiny dried out tendrils of what was once a healthy etiolated root. A dying plant – being aerobic would leave traces of adenosine triphosphate in the soil, he knew, leeched from the root system, which takes place in glycolysis where the cytosol cells break down to eventually create fermentation, but there were no traces according to readouts from the droids, so what was going on, he wondered?

There were no footprints – he deduced that rapidly – deleting the possibility of deer stripping the tree and chomping it up, scanning the soil; the drones careful not to disturb anything as they minced about – knowing something was amiss, but unable to ratify the problem in their own limited mechanical way.

Rulelis dismissed most of them, returning them to their work, instructing those retreating to be a little more vigilant, 'they may well have picked up a hitchhiker during their last survey,' he warned.

He kept two of the robots back to continue in their ministrations and stood askance at the tragedy, a little tearful and more than a tad confused, the once splendid specimen of a grand old age – reduced to so much pulp.

He capitulated wearily, closing to caress the pulpy remains, frowning over the horrid desiccation. Rulelis had a replacement in one of the nurseries but it wouldn't be the same, the younger tree only a sapling.

He ordered the drones to dig up and burn the stump, just in case, and then double check the soil for any impurities, invading insects, or viruses, and get back to him.

He slipped away and consulted the ship's computers through a console in a nearby rest room.

"Computers," he asked testily. "Any sign of any unauthorised movement, other than the wildlife and droids in the domes, or anywhere aboard ship?"

"Affirmative," the security protocol system relayed.

Rulelis was taken back.

"Show," he demanded!

On the screen before him an amorphous shadowy blob whipped across a forest glade, almost faster than the cameras could pan and his vision could comprehend.

"Slow it down," he instructed, and the computer system complied, showing the alien entity in plain view as it sped across open ground.

"What is it," he asked?

There was an interminable pause as the three main computer networks joined forces to confer. At length, they had to admit, there was no available data.

"Could be a ghost, perhaps, from a dead tree," the life support system put in.

"That's ridiculous," Rulelis spat back, "plants, trees, sentient beings are flesh and blood, xylem, water and rhytidome. Even I don't have a soul."

"Any other casualties in that dome," Rulelis posed cautiously.

"Several," stated the security computer system, switching to the dome's cameras.

Rulelis was shaken again; prime specimens denuded, stripped and withered to crumbling mounds, unsightly gaps appearing in a forests' canopy.

"What's doing this," he cried in near panic? "How can I stop it?"

"Sorry," the security systems persisted. "No available data."

"Alright," versed Rulelis. "Implement code one; one; zero nine," and he swept out of the rest room on route for the jungle domes.

***

At dome four he stood at the air lock armed with nothing more than his intellect. It had served him well in the past, having to deal with unruly prehistoric beings who didn't seem to want to know about the wealth of maintaining their world's rain forests on his many travels, so without further ado, he activated the doors and passed through, making doubly sure nothing slipped by him.

In the dome the temperature hit him first, hot and humid, just how all the jungle plants liked it, the towering canopy of giant palms, beeches and brazils, bamboos and oaks, the wonderful snaking vines and alamedas, the radiant moon flowers and succulent ferns. A whole ecosystem here, he mediated, crafted with love and care, a whole biosphere of a world that had long ago blown itself to bits. And now he had an interloper and not only that a destructive one as well!

It would have to go.

Rulelis stalked the paths and glades, wandering through the forest, stopping occasionally to admire an epiphyte or shrub, pleased by the showy violets and orchids. Then, upon emerging from the underbrush, he caught his intruder red handed, almost confronting it as it raped a small bush, reducing it to dust.

"You won't find me so tasty," Rulelis called, bracing himself.

The alien spun round angrily, yellow slits of eyes glowing in an amorphous shape. It regarded Rulelis with contemptuous scorn and after a quick appraisal moved in on him menacingly.

Rulelis steeled himself, holding his ground, preparing for his demise, but hoping his mind might be able to outwit his opponent.

He was unlucky, the entity swamped him quickly, although Rulelis tried to duck aside, the being meshed with frightening speed, engulfing him, stifling his leaves.

"Droids," coughed Rulelis in alarm!

He fought for breath, fretting and twisting and turning, his stomata blocked, crying out for oxygen, and although he thrashed with all his might, the alien held him securely, beginning to drain the life from him, pulsing with voracious tenacity, the spider sucking dry the fly; he battled on, despite the vice-like hold: Endeavouring to meld with it somehow and overcome its thoughts, but it was without empathy, compassion, a bludgeon of a thought wave, wanting only to survive and procreate. Their minds locked in a titanic battle but Rulelis was losing, as his oxygen-fed brain started to fade. His whole body went into shut down mode, abscisic acid pouring through his system. Fronds unfurled and shot out from his body with desperate urgency unleashing indehiscent seeds as the lack of aerobic respiration choked him. He struggled and wrested with the alien but the powerful entity invaded his molecules spreading through him with acidic osmosis. Rulelis experienced the heady sensation as ethylene flushed his damaged parts, acting as a primary trigger to induce the cellulase enzymes to degrade the cell walls; his many external petioles closing down.

He was dying he realised, as his leafy body imploded yet again, buckling under the onslaught, unable to save his beloved gardens he cried out in sheer distress but no-one could help, the surrounding droids unsure of what to do.

"Droids," he squeaked, "save the gardens…"

They spun and chit-chattered to themselves but although they flayed about urgently there was nothing tangible to arrest.

They circled the avatar as Rulelis choked and spluttered his last, whistling and chirping, but he was fading.

One last choking scream… and the mandrake shrivelled.

The entity let a carbonised dust fall from its grasp. It turned to consider the droids then dismissed them and continued on its murderous rampage.

***

Deep in the ship, a carrier wave emergency code awakened an engine; the machine swung out an arm; selected a vial, spinning it around in the vacuumed laboratory, to unleash the enclosed spores onto a rich leaf mould.

Within days the mandrakes would germinate, and then under especial growth hormones and optimum light, moisture and heat, would develop quickly, replacing Rulelis.

From the seed banks, replacement trees and bushes would be ordered.

Eradication of the entity was declared.

Meanwhile, the combined computer systems of the ship noted the loss of Rulelis with a small annotated plaque.

155

-----The End-----

ADAM'S CALLING

Adam woke slowly.

Like two gigantic arms wrestling for supremacy, his subconscious battled with his struggling mind and finally yielded, letting go of his dreams; allowing his consciousness to drift upward; spiraling through his muddled memories – paddling frantically in the last few seconds to the surface where they bobbed about for a moment in a murky sea of ambiguity – waves of confusion and doubt hovering.

'Where the hell am I,' Adam wondered?

He realised next with a jolt that his strong arms were wrapped lightly around a young woman; his fingertips absently exploring the slight bulge of her abdomen, the other hand holding a taut breast.

He relaxed and tried to think, his face buried in her luscious, freshly washed hair, enjoying her scent; detecting a faint aroma of perfume from her neckline.

'Where had he been last night,' he thought? Then remembered vaguely… the pub; the lonely walk home across fields.

Had he wandered into the village – crashed a party or someone's house?

A lone thought, wandering about in his mind like an aberrant vagary, tried to tell him something, Adam mildly shocked to discover it was his own name.

'Well…' he mused. *'I know who I am, so who's this?'*

Something else arrested his attention next, worry beginning to creep into his soul like hot water.

'Was it the weekend,' he asked himself? Endeavouring to recollect anything – the panic to scramble out of bed for work slowly dissolving as he worked his way back and realised; *'Yes! Yesterday*

must have been Friday night; he'd had plenty of money on him!'

Adam capitulated, thinking it must have been some night, stretching languidly; congratulating himself on his conquest. He found however he couldn't recall a damn thing about it, or meeting the girl in his arms, who she was – or where indeed they were – although it felt he'd enjoyed a beer or two from pressure building in the outer hemispheres of his brain – threatening a tad of a hangover.

His throat was dry.

Adam – executing a top to toe mental stock take – realised he felt remarkably sprite however; lasciviously so!

He breathed in again deeply, his senses mingling with the gorgeous scents of his partner, not recognising the milieu of the room, the atmosphere fresh; tinged almost with ice; as if someone had left a window open all night and it was in fact winter.

It was obvious he had stripped off before diving into bed, his boxer shorts all that he appeared to have on, his throbbing erection doing its level best to push the elasticised material out of the way and get to it, but the young woman had retained a little more decorum, retaining her jeans and top; Adam's hands exploring the firm round breast and the gap between the jeans and her pelvis; his fingers sinking to explore the first wisps of pubic hair.

His paramour moved seductively in her sleep, wriggling her hips suggestively, pushing against him – Adam suddenly enlivened, all at once chomping at the bit; an insatiable urge to tear her clothes off – the desire of copulation, seizing him.

Groping hands woke her; the young woman freezing for a moment, as if a waking recollection had startled her: Adam, using the pause to try and collect his own thoughts again, found there were still horribly big holes in his memory: The night before; his lover; the room – now that he had opened his eyes fully – was alien to him, looking a little like the inside of a plane or a shuttle; the ceiling way above, indistinct, as if made of a milky misty substance.

Still; it seemed early and his loins were close to bursting – and if she was willing, then there'd be no holding back – he'd nail her to the wall!

The desire to mate spurred him on; Adam pushing aside any other concerns for the moment, gripped by an inconsolable passion, sunk his face into her neck, nuzzling her; coaxing her; practically tearing at the clasp to her jeans –

Her hand found his!

She turned; her shoulders rolling slightly in his arms, her long black hair spilling from her face to reveal a profile; Adam liking immediately the flash of hazel green eyes as he glanced down – smiling eyes with long luscious lashes, a small straight nose.

"I would usually like to pass a few words of introduction before you jump on and start banging away," she voiced, letting the statement hang in the air for a moment!

Her voice, angel-soft, multifarious; was issued husky with drowsiness.

Adam sighed inwardly, thought for a long moment.

"Morning, I –"

"That'll do," she laughed coyly!

He tore at his boxer shorts in a frenzy; the young woman sliding off her jeans and thong – tossing them aside – ripping off her top to discard it out and over the duvet; snuggling down to turn to him.

He looked deep into those emerald-flecked, hazel eyes, smiling at the pretty face before him, entranced by the rosebuds beneath, bringing the quilt up and over his back as he positioned himself, falling into her arms.

He'd never known such a forceful coupling. Adam surprised at his unbridled ardour, entering her clumsily, lifting her buttocks as he began thrusting away like a machine, an uncontrollable passion exploding in his id, his mind centred on one thing; procreation.

The young woman rose to each occasion, egging on his unrelenting urgency, his pounding hips, meeting him with almost every orgasm; a libidos murmur here; a lustful gasp there – her legs forced up – opened like a pair of scissors; sideways – on her knees – Adam grasping and kneading her breasts as if it was his last act; his lover desperate to sit astride him – her lips crushing his – as energetic as he; ravenous; hedonistic: the boundaries thrown aside.

They teased; romped; played – explored – intimately discovering the other's body; rejoicing in the other's form; gasping; laughing; rolling – trying everything in their imagination; and in their uninhibited state of mind, drank so deep of their tellurian union.

A short breather; and Adam was at her again, like a man possessed. It was as if he'd gone without it for so long, he couldn't stop, now he got the chance; his hormones ignited; his glands rejuvenated; his testes refilled: enthusiasm driving him on – Adam finding himself swelling as if he'd been impregnated with the force of several bulls. The young woman gasped as he ravaged her again, doing his best to be careful but verging on the edge of savagery, he ploughed into her, lifting her like a rag doll once her energy was spent, grinding out the very last of his wanton desires as he reached his third and final climax.

Adam rolled off, catching his breath, his pulse hammering in his veins, stunned at his brutal lovemaking, his partner curling into a crumpled heap, her hair plastered back from her face, her body quivering.

He felt immediately apologetic, propping himself up on an elbow to put a hand tenderly to her shoulder.

"Ok," he asked softly, the inquiry more than a little hopeful, Adam sliding his left arm under the bolster to caress her, holding her tight, moving awkwardly as his member remained a steaming ramrod?

Sleep, a lassitude overwhelmed the both of them, the raging mists of sexuality finally clearing.

Adam, frankly amazed at his stamina, closed his eyes and dozed, his arms wrapped tightly around his paramour.

***

He sprung awake a while later, somewhat conscious of the passage of time, still unsure of his past, his mind verging on the edge of alarm until an underlying calm seized him yet again, the overriding notion that he was on holiday perhaps, staying his hand, filling him with irreproachable relief.

Adam frowned at the lack of responsibility, letting a wayward optimism rule the hour. He put a hand to his forehead, as if to hold in manually the short-term memory that had lodged there, shocked at the avid and rampant lovemaking. *'He'd been a madman,'* he thought berating himself, *'a wild three-shot repeater'*.

He dropped his arm, exhausted; the girl breathing heavily in the crook of his other – as perplexed, he stared at the incandescent roiling ceiling above; an aberrant notion – like the thinnest filament of a thought skittering over his cerebellum – reminding him that he hadn't even got as far in the scant introduction to ask her name.

He was appalled at his callousness.

He rolled to her, lifting a hand tenderly to see if she was awake, a sleepy murmur indicating he had roused her.

"Erm… this might sound a little crass, but I don't know who you are…?"

He shuffled round, struggling back onto his elbow, bending his head to gaze down at her; intrigued by the look of consternation on her face. She was searching for an answer, the worry turning to outright frustration as she struggled to recall the slightest memory of the previous night, anything in fact that linked her to the present, the young woman pushing herself upright; staring into the space before her as the amnesia blocked every conscious recollection.

'*What in God's name was she called,*' she virtually asked herself?

"I'm Jane – I think," she responded at length, "… it began with J – I'm sure?"

"What's yours," she enquired suddenly, turning to gaze at him out of the corner of her eye?

"Adam…"

"You sure?"

Adam nodded to himself, convinced.

The woman turned away, considering their surroundings, a little conspicuous in her nakedness.

"*This your place?*"

Adam shook his head thoughtfully. "Huh?"

"If it's not yours, whose is it then?"

"*Beat's me…*"

Adam cringed as he untangled himself and sat up slowly, swinging his legs over the edge of the bed, his manhood a tad sore for the first time in his life, turning his head to wonder at the neatly folded pile of clothes on a chair next to him; his boots tucked tidily beneath. Not like him at all, to waste time folding up his clothes before diving into bed with a hot little totty.

He put a hand to his head, desperately searching his memory, racking his brains for a semblance of recollection; a scene; an outdoor vision; a path; the façade of a house – a flower bed or hedge he might have floundered in. But nothing came, the party – if he'd been at one, after the pub, the taxi or drive home, getting inside, wherever *'here'* was, had evaporated – Adam unable to recall such a bad state of memory loss in ages; snippets of conversation; shards of elation or disappointment, usually something, but nothing came, his mind an unwholesome void of neural networking that had all but ceased trading.

'This was stupid,' he thought massaging his temple with one set of fingertips, trying to latch onto something that would pin him to the events of last night.

He dropped his hand, the breath catching in his throat, flexing his well-muscled shoulders and casting his vision again around the bedroom, *'or room with a bed in it, to be more precise,'* he thought, for the walls and floor were devoid of any trappings, his surroundings as austere and bland as a blank sheet of paper, the arched opening in a wall a few feet from the foot of the bed, housing toilet and washbasin; seen from his position, another large opening in the room, leading to an open space containing a refractory or kitchen area. Adam was unable to see more at the moment. The window situated in the wall the other side of the bed, at least with two or three sets of net curtaining covering it, might as well have had a brick wall behind it for all the light it gave off, illumination coming from the strange misty ceiling above.

Carefully, Adam got to his feet, his equilibrium re-settling itself as his head wavered a bit, then wandered to the washroom to relieve himself, turning to shut a door that wasn't there, Adam wondering absently if he'd somehow boarded a plane in the night and was now in Alicante or Limogne.

Vacantly, he inspected the washroom. He was in the building trade, although he'd forgotten, but it wouldn't have taken an expert to pick up on the shoddy workmanship; the toilet basin thrown in the corner skew-whiff; the washbasin loose; a vanity chest and ottoman just set against the wall – looking as if they'd been dumped there – the plumbing appearing as if an amateur had attempted to do it.

The taps did at least work, Adam throwing cold water onto his face, the toilet flushing too, after he'd used it. No soap, just a small bottle of liquid hand rinse: no bath or shower although there was room for both, and no mirror; Adam dabbing down his thick brown hair with his hands.

He found towels in an ottoman and wiped his face and hands dry, still trying to remember something of the previous night, still rather abashed over the unbridled passion that had erupted in him earlier, the insatiable carnal yearning of his paramour as well, the girl almost as lustful and preternatural as he.

'Who was she? Where on earth did he meet her?'

He finished up, and strode back into the bedroom, casting a glance side-ways into the atrium/dining area, an open-plan and functional kitchen making him think he'd crashed some interior designers' house, minimalism being the overlying feel; the roiling cloud that was the roof eliciting a thought that it might be a hillside villa, although he couldn't think whose.

Jane, who had slipped on her top, warding off the slight chill that seemed to emanate from the odd ceiling, took her time about sliding to the edge of the bed before committing herself to her feet; Adam mildly shocked as she very nearly buckled on unresponsive legs, her hips feeling as if they'd been disjointed.

Adam moved swiftly to catch her, supporting her lithe frame.

He immediately enjoyed the close contact, cradling her, bending to kiss her lightly on the head, holding her tightly as she collapsed into him.

"Ok," he asked again, happy at their union, Jane being the kind of girl he would have gone for normally, slim, pretty, alluring?

"I guess…I feel as if I've been in a rugby match, but otherwise… Do you think we've died and gone to heaven – or hell?"

"If this is hell, I can handle it."

Strong arms held her, Adam bending to kiss the top of her head again lovingly, respecting the candour and rampant energy earlier, suddenly wanting her again, his ardour rising, his body responding, Jane glancing down and giggling girlishly, turning her face up to him, a coquettish grin playing on her lips.

"You're an animal," she joked, overwhelmed by his energy.

He bit his bottom lip and smiled down at her, her makeup a little smudged; her skin radiant; her oval face streaked with rivulets of sweat; her countenance one of contentment – if a tad weary. She straightened, finding her feet and broke away, blowing him a kiss to spin and pad toward the washroom, eager for a shower or at least a strip wash, the stark bare walls glaring back at her.

Adam, watching her go, admired the shapely hips and backside, fought down the urge to chase after her, desperate to ravage her one more time, ardently damping down his verve, stifling the vagrant daydream that visualised her slim body with all its delights, her ample breasts and shapely legs, his body gearing up for the 'quickie' despite his protestation.

He turned to pick up his clothes to dress, staggered by his insatiable urge to copulate yet again, his loins and manhood seeming to have taken on a wanton life of their own, Adam struggling to do up his jeans as his ardour, impervious to his self-control, vied with his candour.

Finding only one sock predictably, he slipped on his army boots anyway, liking the hard soles and cool tough leather on his feet.

Leaving the laces undone, he stomped through to the refectory, pulling up short to look around: the atrium a long rectangular expanse, was really a kitchen-cum-rest area, a counter/breakfast bar running three quarter's the length of the wall opposite, the area to the right of him a place to chill out, low level circular table and assortment of chairs the only items: no pictures or rugs.

Before him the counter top stretched, equipment lining the wall behind; big American fridges; dishwashers; food processing areas; ranges; cookers: cupboards full of produce; enough for twenty or more people, if needed, Adam realised.

He walked over to inspect the kitchen closer, finding there had been very little thought as to the layout, things thrown in higgledy-piggledy so that a range and fridge were squashed in together with a dishwasher, cooker, and washing machine. Store cupboards, the doors lying open, lined the walls above, stocks of tinned food stacked at random on shelves, no rhyme or reason as to the layout.

He wended his way around the counter to the bar behind, opening and closing the cupboards thoughtfully, pulling open a door to peer into a fridge, finding the same haphazardness pervading the inside, milk lining the door, packets of juice thrown in along with platters of cold meat, packets of cheese and processed foods, salad items and a huge pastry/meatloaf thing that was still in its packet, that one item, enough to feed a party of school children.

Adam reached in for a milk carton, pulling it out to twist off the top and rip off the seal, one sniff telling him the liquid was off, the milk having curdled.

He screwed the lid back on, raising the container to eye level to read the date but the label was smudged and illegible, Adam bending to set it on the floor to one side, to pull out another, finding it was fresh, raising the container to his lips to take a sip, the milk cold and palatable.

The liquid, sliding down into his stomach, told Adam he was more than just a little peckish, and he pulled out the metallic platter of ham, finding another of salmon that he inspected and sniffed several times to convince himself it was all right, finding a pack of cheese biscuits in the cupboard and rooting around for some side plates and cutlery, throwing everything hastily on to the countertop before him.

By the time he'd sliced off some ham and fish, and helped himself to a chunk of the pastry egg and meat roll, garnished two plates with cheese biscuits and a little fresh salad, Jane had freshened up and brushed her hair and was looking absolutely gorgeous as she walked nimbly from the bedroom in her sneakers, dressed back in her tight-fitting jeans; the contours of which stayed Adam's hand as he shovelled meat and fish into his mouth. The young woman was shaking her head, confused over the lack of doors and the bland white walls, the swirling incandescent ceiling.

She stopped at the counter and took a seat on a stool opposite, setting down her handbag, swishing back her hair; appraising the chunky slices of salmon and ham on the plate before her: the small cheese biscuits scattered straight from a box, complimented the fresh salad tossed as a bit of an afterthought, nodding appreciatively; not a terribly good combination, but when in Rome, she thought, smiling at his attempt.

As Adam rummaged and found her some utensils. Jane looked around, eyeing a door to one side of a big arch in the other opposing wall, the opening appearing to go off into a corridor with empty rooms either side, no sound or movement, advertising the seemingly odd apartment was empty.

"Are we totally alone," she enquired, turning back, a little incredulous?

Adam had seated himself again opposite, heartily tucking into his ham and salmon, wolfing it down as if he hadn't eaten for days; the food hardly touching the sides.

"Slow down," she chastised him, "you'll get indigestion."

Adam smiled, not giving up for a moment, Jane's eyes roving over the honed and well-toned muscles in his shoulders and arms, the powerful forearms that seemed borne of hard manual work – either in a gym or building site: his big hands, that had tried to be so tender and careful as they made love over and again only an hour ago, almost glowing with strength; the man before her radiating with vitality and raw energy. The hooded drawstring top, the arms of which had been ripped off some time ago, showed off his bulging biceps, the blue veins standing out in contoured relief against his tanned skin.

Abused and trampled she might be, but she felt her belly tighten, her groin moistened, squirming in her seat as an abnormal amount of serum made its way back down from her cervix, her legs aching from the morning athletics.

'And what a romp it had been,' Jane simpered, almost ashamed and shocked by her own wild lust and libido, the uncontrollable urges!

As she picked up her knife and fork and cut and chewed her food, the unquestioning zeal and desperation with which she had thrown herself into the coupling astounded her, bringing blushes to her cheeks and making her pause and stare straight ahead, the recollection tantalising as it reintegrated itself.

'But where was the rest of her memory,' she asked herself suddenly?

Jane put her cutlery down for a moment, using the break to cast another look around the atrium, the area devoid of any other features apart from a few reclining chairs and a table to the other end of the room, no windows, just a door sitting rather oddly in the opposing wall near the opening to the corridor.

"Can you remember anything of how we got here, Adam?"

Her partner shook his head, having helped himself to more of everything, tucking in hastily, as if he only had a short dinner break in which to eat it all.

'Big engine,' she thought, watching on closely.

"Are we married," she asked suddenly, Adam failing to realise the significance, Jane checking her left hand. "Is this all some kind of joke – *My god"* she spluttered? *"I hope we're not being filmed!"*

Adam nearly choked. He wiped his mouth with the back of his hand, then after pausing to consider her statement, continued munching and chewing, giving the impression however he was mulling things over as he did so, casting his eyes about.

Having finished the biscuits off and crunched ruminatively on two apples, he was apparently sated, shaking his head as he gulped down a quart of milk.

Jane picked at her food sparingly, her face tortured by the loss of recall, Adam taking the plates to the sink to see if he could procure any hot water.

"Why can't I remember anything, Adam? Do you think we were drugged last night?"

He turned thoughtfully from the sink. "Why, what for?"

"Well I'm sure I don't know, but there doesn't seem to be many exits."

He returned and was about to seat himself again; when footsteps from the corridor made the both of them freeze – Adam staring into the face of his partner for a moment.

Jane spun round on her stool, while he slid from the counter to place himself squarely in front of her; Jane, after considering his enormous back sliding off her seat to hang back just at his elbow, as intrigued as Adam at the footfalls.

A myriad set of guesses as to who it might be, and what excuses he might solicit in response to being in someone else's apartment, rushed through Adam's vacuous mind as they waited with bated breath, although he was completely bowled over by the person stepping uncertainly from the arch.

A pretty young woman, of around her mid-twenties he guessed, bedecked in a light blue chiffon skirt and top, stepped hesitantly into the atrium, her short blonde tresses framing a lovely face with soft blue eyes and pouting lips.

Adam folded with relief, not knowing what to expect, it might have been the owner, but due to her hesitancy, it seemed unlikely.

He took a few steps toward her holding out a massive paw.

The woman's gaze alighted on him quickly, her eyes widening with apprehension, a look of outright concupiscence modelling her face next, the woman holding out a hand, as if lost, or unsure of her whereabouts, needing his big strong arms around her.

"I'm Adam," he intoned, the woman stepping quickly into his outstretched arms.

"Where am I," her voice tremulous and sweet?

"You don't know?"

She gazed up at him, tears forming in the bottom of her big blue eyes.

Adam gazed down, his heart melting, his arms tightening around her.

"We don't exactly know where we are either, until now we've been alone here."

"Where's here?"

Adam was at a loss. "I don't know, I'm sorry."

Jane slunk back to her stool, furtively wondering if there was any alcohol on the premises.

'Competition: Just my luck,' she thought.

Adam brought the woman over to the breakfast bar, pulling out a stool for her, seating her a little away from Jane, lingering as the woman kept hold of his hand.

He put his fingertips to her face, caressing the delicate skin for a moment, cherishing the honey-spun strands of hair, enraptured by her beauty, her button nose and sexy legs – more being exposed as her party skirt rode up over her knees. The pretty young woman held his gaze, her soul lifting, her sexuality blossoming.

He'd drunk deep of her heady perfume, fresh and enticing, his manhood reaching new parameters of expansion, his prurience growing tenfold. Perhaps a little kiss –

The bang made the both of them jump, Adam flinching as the magic was broken, the shroud of lust lifting, his mind returning to the present.

He let go of the woman, looking round to Jane who was standing, her arm lying flat on the countertop, a dark look of warning clouding her beautiful aquiline features, her body trembling.

Adam collected himself and stood back, acknowledging the new arrival almost formally, then turning to walk back round to the end of the counter and around to the fridges, putting a reassuring hand out to Jane as he did so, his partner watching him go with annoyance, re-seating herself but facing across to Adam, away from the new woman.

"What's got into you," she had whispered as he passed?

Adam rummaged in the fridge for the orange juice he'd seen earlier.

The fact was he didn't know. He didn't know where he was, or even who he was with, although he was happy at the moment to keep himself busy, wondering just what it was that had gripped him so. He struggled to keep his mind off the new arrival, her perfume inciting a riot with his senses, bringing out a four-pack of the juice and splitting it, ripping one open to slide it with reverence to the woman.

The young lady looked at him oddly, smiling; beguiling; wondering if she should just scoop it up.

"Thirsty," he asked, dreamily, leaning heavily on the counter?

"Glasses, Adam," Jane stipulated, exasperation in her voice?

Again Adam snapped out of his reverie, tearing himself away to duly instigate a search, finally finding a pack in an overhead cupboard and breaking two before getting them out of their cardboard and plastic wrappings, both girls shaking their heads at his impatience.

"So when did you arrive," Jane wanted to know, *"and what's your name?"* She took her eyes finally from her brusque champion, considering their new arrival.

The young woman put down her glass and thought for some moments, her face a picture of doubt and fright.

"I'm not sure. I don't recall arriving. I think I'm called Polly, or is that my budgerigar. Well it will do for now."

"Fact is, I'm not sure of anything!"

"Great! Adam, can you find any wine or booze of any kind? I'm dearly in need of a drink."

"Is this your place, Adam," Polly asked, unable to keep her eyes off his bulk, Jane seething with every indiscretion?

"Nope. We found ourselves here just like you, a few hours ago."

Adam ransacked the cupboards, his frustration at the incongruous situation starting to distinctly annoy him, finally discovering a box of white wine under the sink, bringing it over to the counter to break open.

"Halleluiah," retorted Jane!

Polly moved nearer, unable to hide her interest in Adam, arranging herself by checking her scant makeup in a compact and brushing her hair quickly, throwing everything back into her handbag and setting it to one side, eager to join in the fun, the activity an excuse for her apparent memory loss.

Adam handed Jane a glass of wine, his paramour reaching over to take hold of his fingers as he did so, endeavouring to look deep into his eyes, reinforcing the union they had just shared only an hour ago, Jane flabbergasted that he could even have the temerity to consider another girl in so short a time.

Adam gave her a reassuring smile, but she saw in his eyes the suspicion of doubt seeping through the levity, as if left alone for just one moment he'd be all over the new arrival.

She tried to chastise him with a frown but Adam was blinkered, his own mind a kaleidoscope of visions and shards and snippets of voices and scenes, as if his declarative memory had been a solid object that had been dropped, smashed into a million pieces, only now desperately trying to reformulate itself, one or two icons of sense or recollection of a past beginning to shine through, the frustration building though, his ire simmering just under the surface.

As the women passed pleasantries, Jane pressured into having to make conversation, Adam strode from the counter to the arched opening in the wall opposite; the women watching him go, twisting in their seats to look at each other enquiringly.

He wandered down the corridor opening the doors to the three rooms finding the same arrangement in all of them, en suite bedrooms, double beds, small chest, no openings or windows – no exits, they were completely self-contained. He checked the end of the corridor but it was solid and unyielding, poking his head into the other three rooms on his return journey, re-entering the atrium and stopping to turn back and look at the door in the wall up and down, finding nothing particularly unusual about it.

He took hold of the handle and tried to pull it open, finding the door locked tight.

Adam put his weight into it, leaning with his left hand in case he could catch hold of the edge as he pulled, the wood putting up some resistance until he'd clawed his fingers at the edge, heaving on the door knob, the squealing and splintering of timber filling the atrium as the door reluctantly gave way.

Adam tore it from its mooring, the joints breaking with the creak of wrenching mortise and tenon, his huge arms ripping it asunder, a rush of air gushing past him to evaporate into the room.

A milky effervescent mist confronted him, looking as if he was staring into the worst peasouper he'd ever seen, the sparkling fog glaring back with supernatural force.

Adam set the door to one side, brushing himself down to stare again into the misty expanse before him, the swirling mist not made of water droplets, he realised as he waggled his outstretched fingers in it, but something else, smoke maybe, although it seemed to be alive almost as if it was tangible, thick enough almost to grasp. Spirals curled around his hand as he reached further in, groping to find something, twisting his hand about experimentally.

He pulled it back and inspected it closely, finding his hand was bone dry and still operational, then at a total loss, he walked back to behind the counter, the girls watching on closely, picking up the carton of sour milk he had set aside earlier, carrying it back to the open doorway and without preamble, launching it, the carton sailing into the mist and being swallowed up instantly.

Adam waited, cocking an ear, listening for a thump or crunching splat to sound out, but nothing, just an eerie silence, the swirling mist having swallowed the carton up without a hiccup, scintillating back at him with mute blandness.

'*Well*', he thought, after a moment's serious contemplation, '*that answers one thing: it was no point leaving it open*', Adam picking up the shattered door to push it back in, thumping it home with the flat of his palm, the door looking decidedly worse for wear.

"Are we locked in," asked Polly tremulously?

Adam, about to return to the girls, paused, startled by the sound of a door opening in the corridor.

He turned to peer into it.

Along the corridor a door had definitely been pulled ajar, Adam detecting movement behind it.

Intrigued he walked down toward the room, glancing into one off to his left where a rumpled bed showed where Polly had obviously come from, reaching the door and pushing it open, surprised to find another stunning woman behind it, looking a bit miffed and flabbergasted, her confusion dispelled as she turned from the bed to clap her eyes on him, her surprise and appreciative gaze overturning her anxiety. She appraised the strong broad features, the strapping height, shock of thick brown hair; eliciting a raunchy grin as she reached for him without another moment's thought, this woman apparently in no doubt about her bearing.

She was beautiful, Adam realised, noticing after an appreciative perusal of his own, that she was another kettle of fish altogether from the last two; totally buxom, he cogitated, admiring her ample bosom, child-bearing hips. As she waltzed into his bulging arms, her black ringleted hair wild and tossed back, the trappings seemed to be one of a gypsy perhaps, or biker, Adam liking her forthright bearing and calm demeanour right off, especially the obvious abundance of chest.

She wasted no time, clawing at his jeans with one hand whilst undoing her own with the other, straining to stretch and mash her lips with his, Adam suddenly gripped in the fervour of lust and wild abandon, tore at her top and bra releasing her ample breasts.

"Bed," she murmured, throwing herself onto it, spreading her legs before Adam had even struggled out of his pants.

He had dived into the pool of euphoria without a second thought, hormones raging, ramming his way into the woman like a vengeful demigod, pumping for all he was worth; the woman gasping in excitement and electric pleasure as their bodies united, thrusting against each other, rising quickly to a gigantic climax, the woman crying out in sheer ecstasy, tears flooding her eyes.

Adam roared with his ejaculation, his muscles tightening like a drawn bow… and then he was lost, the explosion almost breaking the bed.

***

Jane could stand it no more, she gulped down her third big schooner of wine in succession having hugged the box, slamming the empty vessel down at the climatic cries and groans emanating from the hallway, almost snapping the stem of the glass, stamping through to what had been their bedroom, satisfying just one niggling issue, the window.

She had considered it earlier, wondering if it would be her escape from this hellhole, the hope that her and Adam were partners obviously wrong, the guy just out to get laid as many times as he could in one weekend.

'Party over! This girl was out of here.'

Only the window was a disappointment, Jane pulling back the curtaining to find it was shut fast and anyway contained the same swirling mist behind it, the same bottomless expansive void Adam had opened the wooden door to, making her feel as if she were atop a mountain or adrift in the stratosphere, or God forbid in a spaceship – her mind reeling at the concept.

Back in the living area, Polly was sitting disconsolately, Jane musing acidly when it was going to be her turn as she flounced back to grab another drink, throwing it down, then stalking straight down the corridor, checking each room for an exit, and finding none, stopping for an instant at the room Adam had occupied, catching sight of a semi-naked woman rising from a bed as she gently teased open the door, her pendulous breasts soaked in sweat, the woman staring back at her unabashed.

"A goddamn breeding programme that's what this is," Jane spat, racing back to the atrium, fighting back tears, angry to boiling point, marching to the door in the kitchen to yank it again from its moorings, throwing the pieces of timber aside as it fell apart, and, with a quick look back at Adam, who had warily emerged from the corridor seconds later, leapt into the oblivion; Jane only just hearing a faint yell of terror as Adam dived across the floor after her.

He had very nearly followed, his common sense and self-preservation leaving him for one fleeting moment, Polly rushing to grab him by the arm, heaving him back.

He sat there for some time afterwards, waiting… as if she might return, but in the end, facing the inevitable; reluctantly pushing himself to his feet to replace the ruined door, calculating his losses.

***

Three more women had appeared; Adam's harem complete, greeting them in his own inimical sexual way or with a lame explanation, all the girls though showing a marked resignation at their plight, unlike Jane, dear Jane who'd pandered to the suicidal defenestration. Jane, who somehow seemed especial to Adam; as if a soul partner or life-long friend; berating himself for her loss throughout the rest of his weird day.

A gym had magically materialised at the end of the girls' corridor, clothes, books, electronic gadgets finding their way into cupboards, items that also sneaked into rooms without anybody noticing, Adam retiring that night on his own to what he considered his room, too tired to dwell on the strange and exotic circumstances. He was unable to dispel the feeling of loss however with Jane, unable to shake off the hole it had left, the picture now incomplete, his set unfinished, crashing untidily onto his bed to fall asleep in seconds.

***

In the early morning glow, he assumed one of the women had slipped into his bed during the night, Adam liking the taut stomach and firm round breast, the sensual husky moans...

A smile played on his lips as he explored the lithe body.

"You know, I usually like to pass a few words of introduction before you jump on and start banging away..!"

The End

I hoped you've enjoyed this small compendium of short stories and lengthier novellas. All were a joy to write and I hope the harsh language wasn't too unsettling.
C.E.H.

www.ingramcontent.com/pod-product-compliance
Lightning Source LLC
Chambersburg PA
CBHW021956120726
47992CB00001B/289